Totally Bound Publishing books by Destiny Moon:

Amply Rewarded
All I Ever Wanted

I0542275

ALL I EVER WANTED

DESTINY MOON

All I Ever Wanted
ISBN # 978-1-78184-786-2
©Copyright Destiny Moon 2014
Cover Art by Posh Gosh ©Copyright April 2014
Interior text design by Claire Siemaszkiewicz
Totally Bound Publishing

Published in 2014 by Totally Bound Publishing, Newland House, The Point, Weaver Road, Lincoln, LN6 3QN, United Kingdom.

Totally Bound Publishing is an imprint of Total-E-Ntwined Limited.

ALL I EVER WANTED

Dedication

For B.

Chapter One

At five o'clock I knocked on Monique's door. She lived on the top floor of a beautiful A-frame house from the early 1900s with two bedrooms and a wrap-around balcony. She was definitely the envy of our group of friends that have stayed together since high school, and she knew it. She didn't show off about it, but when we had a girls' night, it was always at Monique's.

"Darling," she said as I entered. "You are right on time. The pinot grigio is in the kitchen breathing."

"There's a strange use of personification."

"Don't be nerdy. I took the cork off so that the air will bring out the flavor."

She took my coat and tossed it on her antique chair by the door. Then she grabbed my hand and led me to her bedroom.

"I have big plans for you, missy."

"Oh?" I smiled.

When Monique had a plan, there was no point in resisting it. She has great taste. So last week when she'd called and announced she was giving me a makeover, I hadn't wanted to get in her way. Deep down, I needed this. I needed pampering. It had been so long since I'd gotten dressed up or gone anywhere. It was a struggle to get my boyfriend, Pete, out to anything other than the cheap beer and wings night at the pub across the street.

Monique's bedroom was full of designer dresses and tailor made clothes that fit her perfectly. Although our builds were a little different in that she was taller and slimmer than me, I have been known to fit into some of her clothes. On the bed, she had lain out three different dresses, all of them silky and bright. The colors were bold and intimidating.

"Pick one of these. I'll be back with the wine."

I was immediately shy. I lived in my jeans and sweaters when I wasn't at home in my jammies. Looking at the dresses, I panicked. It had been way too long since I'd shaved my legs or tweezed my eyebrows or any of the stuff that goes along with wearing revealing, attention-getting dresses.

Monique came back with two glasses, passed one to me. We toasted as she said, "To fabulousness."

I could tell it was meant as a toast to me but I just sipped my wine silently, feeling less than glamorous. This party had seemed like a good idea in theory at the time I accepted the invitation, but I had more research to do, more books to read and a huge deadline looming.

"Monique, I'm having second thoughts about this. I don't think I belong in your crowd." I sat down next to the dresses on her bed like I used to when we were teens hanging out in each other's room.

"Nonsense! And anyway you agreed. Remember?"

"Yeah, but…"

"No but. You're going." She stroked the middle one, a hot pink satin number that Marilyn Monroe would have loved. "I think you should wear this one."

"It's so not me," I protested.

"How can you say that?" she asked. "It's totally you. You used to live for hot pink, remember?"

"That was so long ago," I said wistfully.

"Seriously, Claudia, do you even know who you are anymore?" Monique shook her head at me like she was trying to get me to acknowledge something.

"What do you mean?" I was taken aback by her tone.

"I mean, don't take this the wrong way. I love you. But have you taken a good hard look at yourself lately?"

"Um…" What was she getting at?

"All right, look. I'll be the one. None of your other friends will tell you so I'll take the risk that you'll hate me but remember, I'm saying this because I love you."

"What is it?"

"You used to be different. Don't you remember? You used to be that fun girl who read fashion magazines and went for pedicures and Bellinis. I haven't seen that girl in ages."

"Yeah, I'm doing a PhD. I don't have time for fashion anymore."

"Can you even hear yourself right now?"

I looked at her, incredulous.

She continued, "It's not about fashion. It's about fun. It's like the joy has gone out of your life or something. I'm worried about you."

I felt naked. Who did she think she was to tell me this? But in my heart I heard her loud and clear. There are some things only a best friend can say.

"When's the last time you treated yourself to a new outfit?" she persisted.

"Uh...I guess it's been a couple of years."

"It's been five."

"You noticed?"

"Yeah. I remember because we went shopping together and after you bought that outfit, you said you were going to hide the receipt from Pete because he didn't like you spending money on clothes."

"It's true. He doesn't."

"Claudia, let me ask you something. Do you love him?"

"Yeah."

"Do you want to marry him? Do you see him as the father of your children?"

I hesitated. "Pete's not exactly the marrying kind and he's nowhere near responsible enough to have children. Besides, we're both focused on our careers right now."

I didn't tell her that I was also footing the bills at home. Pete's income consisted of his student loan, and mine came from the paltry sum I got as a teaching assistant in the English Department at the university. Before Pete and I could even consider having children, we'd both have to finish our degrees and find academic work. I was close to finished, but he was still years away. I couldn't explain that to Monique, who'd been out of school with her loans paid off for years.

"I know you take care of him," she said, as though she could read my mind. "And as your best friend, I need to ask who is taking care of you?"

"I am."

"You can honestly tell me that you love him and see a future with him?"

Suddenly, I realized that my best friend knew me better than anyone and that she could see right through me. She didn't believe my lies. She had known me for way too long. The financial pressures at home had been getting to me for months. There was no end in sight. That was just one small aspect. Pete and I had been growing apart for a while now. I'd come to resent his idealistic resolve to throw himself into his studies without working. It'd been ages since he'd taken a shift at his old job with a catering company because he found it demoralizing.

"It's that obvious?" I started to tear up. I was sick of him, tired of his excuses and our life together.

"Look, he's a nice enough guy. Don't get me wrong. It just feels like you're in a rut on a lot of levels."

I was full on sobbing. Pandora's Box was open and it was time to let the secrets out. We both put our wine glasses down on her dresser and she held me. I had to stop lying to myself, had to stop trying to convince myself that everything was fine when it wasn't.

"Oh, Monique," I whimpered. "You have no idea how good it feels to finally admit this. We turned into Burt and Ernie or something. We never go out on dates anymore. He never does anything sweet. I don't put in effort either. You should see my bush right now. I'm a hairy beast and I don't even care."

She laughed as she rubbed my shoulders. "That's not right."

"I know."

"Claudia, you are a sexy woman. You always have been. Don't you remember how guys used to hit on you whenever we went out?"

"That was ages ago."

"But you remember, right?"

I assented. We did used to have a lot of fun at nightclubs in our early twenties, during our undergraduate years. Even then, Monique had been in business and I had been in literature so our crowds had been completely different, but I used to tag along with her on Friday or Saturday nights. She had done my makeup and lent me club clothes and it had been a ton of fun. She was right. I hadn't done anything fun for ages. Being saddled with domestic responsibility had left me feeling as sexy as a dishcloth.

"I'm frumpy," I sobbed, putting my face into my palm. How had my life completely unraveled over a single glass of white wine? "You're right, Monique. I'm in a rut."

"You're not. Well, okay, you have been. But tonight, we are killing Frumpzilla and restoring the real you. All right?"

"Yes," I chirped.

"Good. You can deal with your relationship afterward, but you can't see anything clearly until you take care of yourself."

"Yes, ma'am."

She passed me a towel and took me to her bathroom. "Now get in there and shave your legs and pits and trim your bush. We've got a party to go to."

I couldn't help but laugh at Monique's blunt words. Under her tutelage, I was able to scrub off the bad layers and emerge light and carefree. Frumpzilla was about to vanish and from that moment forward I was determined to get in touch with my old self. In Monique's shower, I lathered up with her decadent rose and neroli scented scrub and the sensual experience consumed me. How had I forgotten that a girl needs a good scrub and shave now and then?

Taking care of myself was divine. My own shower was filthy. Pete and I constantly argued over whose turn it was to clean — which resulted in it never getting done. So, I rarely indulged my desire to be pampered in the shower. Here, in Monique's newly renovated bathroom with a detachable showerhead, it was so easy. I washed my hair with her Aveda shampoo that smelled fantastic. I couldn't help but get turned on watching myself transform. Looking down at my freshly shaven legs, I saw that the fun-loving girl I'd neglected was still there.

I decided I better shave my bikini area as well so I lathered up like I was in a porn scene and it was awesome. I ran the razor over the foam and the smooth skin beneath. Monique's shower had a small ledge that I was able to sit on. I did something that I had not done in a long, long time. I switched the water flow option on the detachable showerhead to 'massage' and let the pulsating water stream run over my pussy. I fingered myself. My pussy was totally wet, inside and out. I parted my pussy lips just a little and let the pulsing water hit my clit. It threatened to send me over the edge, which seemed inappropriate since I was in my best friend's shower. I knew I had to do this, that it was an important step in actualizing the new and improved me. I squeezed my nipples with my right hand while holding the showerhead with my left, and as soon as I gave into my body's craving, I was engulfed in the warm sensuality of the water's flow. My pulse quickened. My nipples were so hard, and my clit couldn't take the pressure anymore. I reached down and touched the wetness.

I turned the water off and toweled myself dry. I was flushed, like I'd just had sex, which I supposed I had.

* * * *

Monique, who was already in her dress that looked like a silk scarf tied in two spots, was applying foundation at her mirror as I came into her bedroom.

"Massage option, eh?"

"Um." I blushed. "You heard that?"

"Yeah." She winked. "That's my girl."

Then, as I walked by her, she playfully spanked me. She was hilarious that way, so free and fun to be around.

Monique was the kind of best friend who liked knowing this stuff about me. In our first year at the University of Toronto she had wanted to know what it was like to kiss a girl and she'd chosen me. It was in her dorm room. She'd just leaned in and planted it on me. Then, when the initial shock had worn off, I'd kissed her back. We'd spent about an hour making out and both of us had been so turned on. I think we could have taken it further but we'd held back. After all, we had been friends for ages and in the back of my mind I was already having a hard time explaining it to our gang. I don't remember who pulled away first, but I've often wondered what could have happened if we had continued. Maybe she wondered, too. We've had a special bond ever since.

I got dressed. The pink satin felt so smooth against my skin. With all my senses heightened from my orgasm, I was in heaven. I took a sip of wine, sat on Monique's bed to watch her apply the finishing touches of makeup.

"You look gorgeous," I said.

"Thanks. This mascara is new. What do you think?"

"It's sultry."

"I hope Jerome thinks so, too."

"Trust me. He will. So what's going on with him?"

"Well, nothing. I want to torture him after he had me transferred to his colleague's department."

"He probably couldn't stand to be around you because he wanted you too badly."

When Monique was finished with her own makeup, she did mine. She pampered my face with primer, foundation, powder and eyeshadow, liner, mascara and lipstick. She even tweezed my eyebrows. Her treatment was the equivalent of about a year's worth of counseling sessions in terms of how it made me feel. I was floating. I'd come in a heavy rock and turned into a kite. I vowed then and there that Pete was going to have to accept this new side of me. He was going to have to accommodate my inner glamor girl or else I'd send him packing. Monique was right. At twenty-seven, a girl needed to get choosy.

Our flirty and fun banter continued well into the cab ride there. It was good to have Monique to get my confidence up. On my own, I didn't think of myself as hot. Pretty, maybe. Monique treated me as though I was some kind of blonde bombshell knockout, and I had to admit that her dress, her shoes, my freshly shaved legs and pussy were all combining to make me feel spectacular. Monique had also curled my hair and had insisted on liquid eyeliner, so whenever I caught a glance of my reflection in the window, it was hard to believe I was still the same person.

We pulled up to the Royal York, and I followed Monique inside. The lobby was splendid and glitzy, everything my daily life was not. I wanted to stop and admire the massive chandelier and the winding staircases that seemed like they'd been transported from the set of *Gone With the Wind*, but Monique looped her arm in mine and led me to the left. We saw a poster board with the words *Porter & Sons* in calligraphy. The door to the ballroom burst open and two executives exited the party. Although they were mid-conversation with each other, both of them made eye contact and bowed vaguely, addressing us. "Evening, ladies," they greeted.

Monique was already peering into the room trying to make her assessment. She was always a few steps ahead in social situations, and I was grateful she took the lead. My critical inner voice told me I was playing dress-up.

Immediately, she spotted her new boss across the room. She was drawn toward the center, which was a challenge. I'd have been happy to stay in the corner a little longer to gain some perspective, but I was on Monique's arm.

"Perfect," she whispered. "I'll introduce you to my boss. I don't see Jerome yet but let's assume he can see us."

She sashayed up to Hugh who gave her a kiss on each cheek and told her she looked lovely. I followed close behind. He extended his hand to me.

"Hugh," he introduced himself.

"Claudia."

His grip was firm. He was a handsome guy, mid-forties or so. "So glad you could join us." He looked into my eyes.

I felt nervous, suddenly aware that I was pretty out of my element at a place like this. It was not exactly beer and wing night at the pub.

"Excuse me," Monique said. "I have to go say hi to Jerome."

With that, she was gone and I was left to talk with her boss. *Awkward.*

"So how do you know Monique?" he asked.

"We go way back. High school," I said.

"My, that is a long time. Well, maybe not for you. You look very young, if you don't mind my saying."

"I don't mind at all," I told him. "I'm actually twenty-seven, though, so I'm not exactly a spring chicken."

He laughed. "Well, I'm forty-six, so I would beg to differ. You are most definitely a spring chicken."

I blushed, even though his comment was very corny. It had been so long since a man had paid any attention to me that even though Hugh was not exactly a courting genius, I was flattered.

Just then, another man in a suit came up and joined us. He appeared to be younger than Hugh but had that manly confidence that business guys have. At the university, I hardly ever saw that type. He was dressed in dark gray, which suited his features and the silver highlights above his ears. His gaze was forceful, and I relished the attention he gave me. It was foreign yet intoxicating.

"Introduce me to your friend," he said to Hugh, taking my hand and kissing the back of it.

I'd entered some kind of time warp where men actually acted like characters in Jane Austen novels. I was not used to this. The striking stranger held onto my hand a little longer than seemed usual, not that I would know.

"I'm Claudia," I said. "I'm here with Monique."

He looked inquisitively at Hugh.

"My assistant in the PR department."

"Ah"—he turned his attention back to me—"I'm Sebastian. It's a pleasure to make your acquaintance."

"You too," I said, feeling as though I should have brushed up on business etiquette. I didn't know how to behave in this environment at all.

"So you don't work with us?"

"No."

"Too bad. You should. It's an excellent company."

I guessed he was joking but I was floored by his confidence. He didn't know anything about me. Had he been less charming, I'd have been infuriated. As it was, I found myself deeply enchanted by this handsome stranger.

"So I hear," I said.

"Come with me," he said, taking my arm in his. "Let's get you a drink."

I looked at Hugh, not knowing quite what to say. It seemed terribly rude to ditch my friend's boss but Hugh bowed in my direction.

"You don't mind if I steal her away for a while, do you?" Sebastian asked Hugh perfunctorily—he was not actually seeking permission.

I had not been aware that I was a thing to be stolen. This was surreal. Yet, this dashing gentleman was so swift with his moves and so elegant, I couldn't help but feel excited to be on his arm. I've never been the girl on someone's arm before. I'd never let Pete lead me anywhere, not that he had tried. We were always side by side.

As we walked across the floor to the bar, Sebastian gave my arm a little squeeze. It was subtle, undetectable to others, but it sent a shock through my system.

"What do you like to drink?"

"I don't know. What's available?" As I'd said it, it had occurred to me that I betrayed my drinking style—I was that girl who'd drink anything offered, anything free. I didn't have standards. In a room like this, with these kinds of people, that felt very wrong and I racked my brain to come up with something fancy.

"Anything you like."

"I usually drink beer but it doesn't go with the dress, does it?" I knew the answer.

"No."

"Gosh, I don't know."

We approached the bar and I didn't know what to ask for. It was a busy function. I was stressed about holding up the line and ready to drop the façade and ask for my usual—a pint of pale ale.

"Chambord and soda," Sebastian ordered. Then he turned and looked into my eyes. "It'll go with your pretty dress."

"Why thank you." I was so relieved to not have to decide.

"My pleasure."

There was magnetism between us, something intense that I had not felt with anyone before. I wondered if it were just my perception. Maybe it was my freshly trimmed pussy sending curious messages to my brain. I had to strain to remember that I did have a boyfriend at home and I did not know this man who had taken it upon himself to order a drink for me. Had Pete ever ordered for me at a restaurant, I'd have slugged him on principle. I had never let him treat me like a lady, never let him be the man. But it wouldn't exactly be appropriate to punch this man in the arm at Monique's company party. I was tempted to point out that I was perfectly capable of taking care of myself, thank you very much, but the truth was, I was titillated by his courteous mannerisms.

The bartender passed a champagne glass with a sparkly pink soda to Sebastian, who handed it to me.

"Pour vous, mademoiselle," he said.

"Merci."

"So, I'm not mistaken? You are a mademoiselle?"

This was too much. How cheesy!

"Sort of." If asked point blank, I had to tell him I was taken but instead, the words that came out of my mouth were, "I don't believe in marriage."

"Hmm. Very wise," he said. "It's not for everyone."

It was so awkward, that moment when he'd said that. His whole demeanor changed for just a split second. And for the first time, I saw the evidence. It had been right there all along—a gold band around his fourth finger. I don't know how I'd overlooked it before. He changed the subject. "So, Claudia, what is it that you do?"

"I'm working on my PhD," I said.

"Impressive. What do you study?"

"Milton."

"I know nothing about him." He looked almost bashful.

"That's fine. I get that a lot."

"And you do well with that?"

I didn't know what he meant by that. "I'm sorry?"

"Does it make you happy?"

"Oh, well, I guess. Milton's not exactly a motivational writer. Cautionary, maybe, but certainly not pleasant to think about all the time. So to answer your question, sure. I'm happy. I used to be, anyway." I was shocked by what I telling this stranger, and knew I wasn't actually talking about Milton but the sum total of my life at that point. I couldn't believe what I'd said. Had I just admitted to someone I barely knew that I'd lost my spark in life?

"Well, life is short. We should do what makes us happy. If it no longer does, perhaps it's time to move onto something new."

"I'm committed to seeing it through. Besides, I'm almost finished. I defend in a couple of months."

"I appreciate a woman who's willing to commit herself to something," he said somewhat flirtatiously. If he hadn't had the ring on his finger, and I hadn't declared that I didn't believe in marriage, I might have misunderstood his remark.

"Um, thanks," I said nervously. "I should probably go find Monique." I was turning the shade of my dress, no doubt. I needed to get out more. I'd become way too sensitive to male attention. I had to end this interaction before making a fool of myself and embarrassing Monique.

"All right. Well, enjoy the party. I'm sure you will. You are the most enchanting woman here."

He kissed my cheek, and before I knew it I was walking away from him even though I didn't want to. I wanted to get to know him better. I wanted to explore our chemistry but it was dangerous. I had not felt that kind of attraction for anyone before and it was not my style to get flirty with a married man.

Nevertheless, his compliment imbued the evening with a sense of wonder. I felt like Cinderella at the ball. Monique and I wound up talking with Hugh again. Monique was schmoozing professionally and turning up the charm. All the while, I couldn't get my mind off Sebastian. I couldn't wait to tell Monique about him, but there was no way I was going to say anything at the event.

* * * *

After the party, we took a cab back to Monique's.
"I can't believe the nerve of Jerome," she said.
"What happened?"

"Well, I walked up to him and he put his arm around me and told me I look beautiful."

"I thought that's what you wanted."

"It was," she huffed. "But I don't know if he meant it. I mean, maybe he was just saying it to be nice."

"Monique, stop it. Look at yourself. You *are* beautiful. He meant it."

"So why did he transfer me and then proceed to ignore me?"

I shrugged. "I don't know."

"Men make me crazy. I just want a real man, someone I can rely on. Someone who treats me with respect and who has goals and ambitions…"

"And is a tiger in bed…"

I'd heard Monique's description of what she wanted a million times so I'd quoted from her list. She didn't seem to mind at all. If anything, it encouraged her.

"…who loves me and allows me the freedom to continue to grow." Monique's voice was noble, like she was giving a valedictorian speech at the school for husband-hunting. "Who respects his mother and grandmother, who doesn't want children and who never cheats or even thinks about cheating."

"Don't forget the part about being drop-dead handsome and ordering clothes from the J. Crew catalog."

Monique laughed. "I know you don't believe me, but my prince is out there and I still think he answers to the name of Jerome."

I put my head on her shoulder and rested there like I used to do when we took the bus after school together. Monique was more than a friend. She was a sister. I didn't want to see her get hurt by Jerome but at the same time, her expectations were so high, I couldn't help but feel envious that she had such high visions. It plagued me as I thought about going home to Pete. My high hope for the evening was that he had done the dishes.

Chapter Two

I changed out of my party gown and, like a real life Cinderella story, went home on the Subway in my jeans and old sweater. Still, beneath my drab uniform, I was shaved and feeling sexy and thought I'd surprise Pete. I could definitely use some release after the intoxicating experience of Monique's world of men. What we needed was a good physical connection. It had been way too long. If we reconnected, I would be able to let go of the conclusions I seemed to have reached a few hours earlier, that the end was near. Why didn't I want to face that? I guess nobody likes breaking up, especially in the midst of so much work. I was only a couple of months away from defending my thesis, after all. I could go a little longer without making dramatic changes. *Sex would solve a lot.*

When I opened the door to our apartment, I got a funny feeling right away. I couldn't quite put my finger on what was off but something was definitely amiss. It was as though it was not my home, as though I was in some *Twilight Zone* apartment that looked just like the one I lived in but with an eerie quality. There was soft music playing and clothes all over the floor. I opened the door to our bedroom and that's when I saw two naked bodies, one of them Pete's. The other I recognized instantly, too. It was Penny, his ex-girlfriend. They froze and stared at me.

"I've seen enough," I said, turning on my heels and walking away.

Pete leaped up and ran toward me, covering himself with a sheet from the bed. "I can explain. Don't go."

"All right," I said, pausing in the middle of the hallway. "Explain."

"I thought you were staying at Monique's tonight."

"That's not an explanation."

"I'm sorry."

"It's over. Get your stuff out of here by the end of the week, leave the key on the kitchen counter and don't call."

"Claudia," he pleaded. "I've nowhere else to go."

"Fine," I said. "I'll leave. This apartment will never feel like home again anyway."

"Claudia," he repeated. "Don't go."

But I was already out the door. The sidewalk that held magic and promise on my way home now stank of garbage. A rat scurried across my path. Everything was disgusting.

Steaming mad, I got back on the Subway and headed to Monique's. I was so confused by what I'd just seen I could barely cry. It was as though I'd been hypnotized. I was in a dream or maybe a nightmare, but I couldn't react to it emotionally. My mind busied itself with the practical elements first, such as where I'd sleep tonight. I was pretty sure Monique had extra blankets, but I hadn't slept over at her place since our undergraduate days. When had Pete and Penny revisited those feelings? I knew they were friends but I thought it was a positive indication of Pete's character that he could be friends with an ex. I should have known. And Penny. She'd been so nice to my face. *What kind of person behaves like that*? Nice on the surface but secretly ready to pounce on an attached man. What a moron I was. *How could such a beautiful evening have turned so ugly? Is it karma for flirting with a married man at the party?* It definitely felt like punishment.

By the time I got back to Monique's, the lights were out. I knocked.

I could see her peer out of the security peek hole. She opened the door.

"Oh my God!" she exclaimed as soon as she saw me. "What happened to you? You look awful."

"I, uh— Can I stay on your couch for a few days?"

"What's wrong?"

"I walked in on Pete and his ex-girlfriend in our bed."

"That pig. Come inside." She whisked me in hurriedly.

"I'm sorry to trouble you. It's late and…" I actually knew it was fine to show up any time. She had done it to me too in the past. It was what best friends were for.

"It's Saturday tomorrow. We can stay up all night if we feel like it. Come on. Let me make you a hot chocolate."

"How could I have been so stupid?" I asked. "I should have known he was getting it somewhere else. He just told me two weeks ago he was totally fine with us not having sex anymore."

"What a liar. You know what? I always hated that guy. I'm sorry. I don't mean to tell you this right now, but he was no good for you."

"You're right. I see it now. It's perfectly clear for the first time."

"You deserve so much better."

We curled up on her couch and watched *The Way We Were* because Barbra Streisand is the best medicine. Monique gently rubbed my shoulders until I fell asleep.

* * * *

I woke up around noon the next day, covered in blankets. If I'd revealed to Sebastian that I'd subconsciously wanted change, well, I had gotten it. It mystified me that the truth had come out like that. His words made so much sense to me—I'd always believed that the goal of life was to be happy, and I had admitted that I was not, both to Monique and to Sebastian. A friend and a stranger. I'd made the realization and clearly so had Pete.

After making me breakfast, Monique said, "You are not going back there until that jerk and all of his trashy furniture are gone."

"Actually, I told him I'd leave."

"What? Why should you leave? He's the one who messed up."

"There's no way that place could feel like home again. Besides, I wouldn't be able to afford the rent without his measly student loan," I said, taking a bite of the omelet she'd made.

"You could get a roommate."

"For a one-bedroom?"

"Or a better job."

"Where? I'm already stretched to the max as a TA. What am I going to do? Moonlight at the burger joint down the street?"

"Well, no. Maybe I could find you a job as an assistant. We could work together. You could move in with me for a while. Think about it. It'll be fun. Just till you get back on your feet and figure out your next move."

"I hate the idea of going back to that place, even just to pack my things."

"So don't."

Monique called my landlord and gave notice on my behalf. Then she called a moving company and gave them instructions. Most of my books would go into storage and my necessary belongings would get put into a suitcase and brought over here. Done. All she said was, "Happy Birthday." It was months from my birthday but I knew what she meant. It was our little inside joke with each other whenever we did the other favors. It meant everything to have a friend like her.

All day, analysis poured out of me. I needed this time with my best friend because she could understand me.

"I felt bad that I flirted with that married guy last night, but you know what? It was refreshing. I haven't had a man pay attention to me in a long time."

"Don't feel bad. I mean, don't go turning into a home-wrecker either. You don't want to do what Penny did to you. But it's perfectly harmless to let men be nice to you. That Pete sure wasn't."

"Was he that bad?"

She nodded. "What did he have going for him exactly?"

"I'm not sure. I can't even remember why I fell for him. It was up at the university. I think we bonded over a meeting about how the department should be run."

Monique made a face of disgust. "You can do so much better."

"I think I got busy with my work and didn't pay much attention at home."

"Don't blame yourself. He was a jerk."

I once read an article about how cheating was a collaboration between both spouses, even if one didn't know it was going on. Somehow both parties in a relationship helped to bring it about, but now that I experienced it, I couldn't believe that I had made it happen. Hadn't I been willing to have sex? In my own mind, I had done everything I could to make the relationship work. But what I had implied to Sebastian at the party haunted me. *I used to be happy.*

"So what married guy did you flirt with last night, anyway, you saucy minx?" Monique teased.

"A nice guy named Sebastian."

"Sebastian Porter?" She looked shocked. Her jaw literally dropped. "He's one of the owners of the firm. And of several others, too."

"Oh," I said, suddenly feeling as though I'd misread the magnetism, like it couldn't possibly have been real between this tycoon and me.

"I'm sure I made too much of it in my own head, anyway. Let's just drop it."

She nodded, as though she was also in disbelief. I wasn't insulted or anything. I was actually kind of relieved to discover he was that far out of my league and not just some middle management cubicle guy looking for a cheap fling.

* * * *

A few weeks later, I had effectively moved to Monique's couch and was in the midst of a premature mid-life crisis. Everything I had built with Pete was gone in an instant but, in a way, it had disappeared slowly. Or perhaps it had never been there to begin with. It had been dreadful getting through the last part of the semester, but I'd painstakingly made my way through nearly one hundred undergraduate papers and given each one a grade and comments. Though I could barely recall a single moment of it because of my nerves, I had got through my thesis defense and it had been a roaring success. My department friends had all shown up for it and had told me afterwards I answered every question brilliantly. Inside, I had been on autopilot. It had felt like my life was falling apart. Sure I knew everything there was to know about *Paradise Lost.* Of course I did. That was my work and work was all I had at that point. I'd managed to avoid Pete completely and although I was tight financially, I was looking forward to the future.

Then, one day, I received a phone call.

"Claudia? It's Sebastian. Listen, I'm in a bit of a bind. You see, my assistant just quit on me for a part in *Rent.* I never should have hired an actor. I know this is quite sudden, but can you do me a massive favor and step in for a week or so?"

"Actually, I can." I could definitely use the money.

"Perfect. Where do you live? I'll have my driver fetch you in an hour and thirty minutes. I need you to come with me to an art auction tonight. We just have to see and be seen so just wear something elegant casual and we can talk business on the way."

"Um, okay."

As soon as I hung up the phone, I wondered what had just happened. I had no idea what I'd just said yes to. I ran into Monique's room and opened her closet.

Thank God she had an inventory of clothes. After a quick shower, I put my hair in rollers, did my makeup, slipped into Monique's black cocktail dress then left her a note on the coffee table.

Looks like your dream is coming true after all. Got a call from Sebastian. I think I'm his temporary assistant. I have no idea what I'm doing. Will tell you all about it tonight. Borrowed your black dress. xoxo, Claudia

I was in the back of Sebastian's Audi when I got a text message from Monique. All it said was—

Call me!

I dialed her number, and she picked up right away. "Are you crazy? He's the head of the company. Bigger, even. He's the heir. This guy is not only the head honcho but like the head honcho and the son of the head honcho rolled into one."

"Calm down," I told her. "He called me. He obviously sees that I'm competent."

"Oh, Claudia. No offense, but be careful. He's married."

"Quit worrying. Don't psyche me out. I gotta get off the phone. I'll see you tonight."

Just then, the driver pulled up to a mansion, and through the tinted windows of the car I saw Sebastian emerge from the front door and make his way down the steps. He was dressed to the nines in black tie attire. Why had he told me to dress casual?

He opened the door and got in beside me. "Good evening, Claudia. You look lovely."

"Thank you. You're dressed so formally. I thought you said elegant casual."

"I didn't want you to stress."

"Will I be dressed appropriately?"

"Most definitely. There will be lots of artists there."

I supposed that he meant there would be people with considerably less money than him there. It occurred to me that he probably had no idea I was such a person. That was the danger of giving off a false first impression.

"So, on our way over, let me explain what I had in mind. I need someone who can help me with certain social functions. My family donates a lot of money to various organizations, particularly the arts, and it's rude to not show up to opening nights and the like, so I need you to take on a bit of a cultural ambassador role. Do you think you can do that?"

"So you want me to be in charge of your calendar and make sure you go to the events you were invited to?"

"Yes, and to handle the correspondences. It gets to be a lot. Like I said, we give a great deal of money away. It's a full time job just to keep up with it."

Whoa. It's going to be my full-time work to stay on top of all the money he gives away and the thank you cards he receives for it.

"Um, I think I can handle that."

"Good. I'd like you to come with me at times, too. You'll get to meet the elites in the arts. I hope you're okay with that. Tonight, you'll have to talk to a bunch of abstract painters. Can you make conversation with them?"

"I love painters. I mean, I love painting."

"Good. This is why I hire assistants from the arts. Makes sense, doesn't it? Most business students have no clue. It's unfortunate. They're not very well rounded, wouldn't you say?"

"I suppose. Though, I could argue that I'm not particularly well rounded in that I don't know much about business."

"Your humility is charming, Claudia. You have a PhD in Literature. I'm sure you know plenty."

"I don't," I stressed. "I'm a TA in the department of literature at U of T. I'm a scholar."

Maybe I should have just listened to Monique. This evening seemed like a bad idea. But there was something about him that I trusted inherently. It's hard to explain that kind of thing. I was at ease around him. Maybe it was because he reminded me a little bit of Tom Hanks, someone you'd put in the good-looking category not because he had symmetrical features or was conventionally handsome but because he exuded kindness and sincerity. If this man was some kind of player, as Monique seemed to think, it would have been a big surprise to me. The way he fiddled with his watch struck me as a manifestation of nerves. Maybe he wasn't nearly as comfortable in crowds and amongst the city's art scene as he was supposed to be, given his status.

I talked with some of the painters and guests and the whole time I could barely remember my own name because I was so nervous, like the world knew something I didn't.

Out of the corner of my eye, I spotted Pete. He was wearing a white shirt and black pants and he had a tray of canapés with him that he was circulating among the guests. He had not spotted me so I turned in the opposite direction and, frankly, bolted to the little girls' room where I locked myself in a stall, called Monique and told her about Pete working at the event. She only laughed.

Still laughing, she finally said, "Karma's a bitch."

"What do I do?"

"What do you mean? Nothing! You revel in it. You're there as a guest—in fact, you're with the guest of honor."

"What if Sebastian asks me about him later?"

"Tell him the truth. He's a guy you *knew*."

"I don't know if I'm cut out for this."

"You can do it."

I put on my lipstick and checked my hair in the mirror. A couple of deep breaths later, I rejoined the party by approaching Sebastian who was in the midst of a conversation with a couple of painters.

Pete walked up to us, wide eyed. He stared at me and gave me the up-down, undoubtedly trying to understand how it was that I was dressed this way, with my hair done and makeup on, and I'm sure he was confused as to why I was there with Sebastian Porter. I could tell he wanted to say something but he couldn't. He was in uniform and I was dressed up and on the arm of this handsome man. He must have been totally stupefied.

Breaking our intense and awkward silence, Sebastian said, "Claudia, would you care for a crab puff?"

"No, thanks," I said. "But those mini quiches look good."

My mute ex-boyfriend watched the whole interaction with an expression that looked like he was witnessing a foreign ritual he did not understand. Pete skulked away after that, tail between his legs, seemingly destroyed. Karma *is* a bitch, I reminded myself. Had *I* not also been hurt by his actions? So I ate my mini quiche and that was that.

* * * *

"Did you have a nice time tonight?" Sebastian asked me on the way home.

"I did," I said. "It was fascinating to see the new exhibit. I especially enjoyed the Claire Verdan paintings. They captured the tumult of the times quite perfectly."

"You think?"

"Well, yeah. The dark purples and reds were so passionate against the stark backdrop of gray. Seeing the pieces together was so powerful."

"Now, this is why I like working with people in the arts. We can actually talk about art. A lot of the financial contributors to the arts don't give a whip about it."

"I wouldn't know," I said.

"Where did you grow up?"

His question made me wonder what he wanted to know.

"On a farm just outside of Kingston. My mom is a playwright and my dad is a journalist so we had a lot of books and they love the arts. I grew up around actors and painters and writers. None of them had a lot of money."

"Artists seldom do. That's why they find benefactors. That's where people like me come in."

He was so unabashed about his wealth, it was almost off-putting but it was strange. He wasn't boasting. It almost seemed a burden to him, like it was his lot in life.

"You seem sincerely interested in art," I observed.

"I am."

"Well, if you grew up privileged, why didn't you pursue it as a discipline?"

"You mean, since I had all that money, why didn't I become a painter? The answer is, I tried. I wasn't that good."

"Oh." My intuition told me I'd cut his heart open and poured salt into it. "Sorry I asked."

"I'm not. You're pretty brazen, aren't you?"

"I say what's on my mind, if that's what you mean."

"I appreciate that," he said.

"So what did you think of tonight's exhibit?" I wanted to know.

"I was impressed. And jealous. We went to art school together years ago. In another lifetime. Claire Verdan is an old rival of mine, actually."

"But you sponsored the event."

"I prefer the word benefactor."

"Oh." The whole scenario unfolding in front of me seemed tragic now. I didn't know how to respond.

"Look, I made peace with it a long time ago. I don't have the talent for painting. I don't have enough to express. Yet my contribution is an important one. Without it, Claire's work could not exist."

"Of course. It's huge. I admire what you do."

It was true. I could see the value of it and suddenly it struck me that Sebastian was a truly humble person to recognize his function in making art happen.

He just nodded and looked out of the window. We drove in silence for a while until he said, "I think I had a mistaken impression of you."

"How so?"

"When I met you at the fundraiser last month, I saw this drop-dead beautiful knockout and I couldn't help but think that such an attractive young thing might be on the lookout for someone to spoil her."

"What?" I was totally offended. The hairs along the back of my neck all stood at attention. My shoulders tensed.

"I was obviously wrong," he said nonchalantly.

"Yes. Very wrong. For one thing, Monique practically made me go. I had to borrow a dress from her. For another, my ex-boyfriend was in attendance tonight. He brought canapés around. I am not a gold digger."

Sebastian looked positively shocked and apologetic. "I didn't mean to imply anything. Forgive me."

"Look, I don't know what you think or what world you're from but I've worked hard for everything I have and, well, I don't have a lot. I'm actually staying on Monique's couch right now."

"Oh dear. I'm sorry. I'm horrible with women."

It was so out of character for me, but it had been a long time since my feelings had surfaced in the form of tears yet now, here they came. I couldn't hold back. Like it wasn't bad enough that I had just got out of that awful relationship with a man who had had a terribly mistaken impression of me, now every man seemed to.

"I knew it was a disaster to go to this event with you tonight. I never should have said yes."

"I'm glad you did. Otherwise I never would have gotten to know you and that would have been my loss."

When things seem too good to be true, they pretty much are.

"Look, just take me home and we can chalk up this whole mess as one big misunderstanding and that's that."

"Are you saying that you don't want to be my assistant?"

I sighed.

"Claudia," he pleaded. "You misunderstood me."

"I think I understand perfectly. You came up with this whole you-need-an-assistant story to manipulate me into spending time with you," I said. Then with a more judgmental tone, I added, "That's messed up."

In that moment, I realized I had a lot of baggage around men and what they wanted. Pete's cheating ran through my head as a reminder that men always seemed to be the same. They all wanted to satisfy their own egos, and I wasn't interested in being used. The rational part of me was reaching for logic. I knew intellectually that Sebastian and Pete were not the same but after a wicked, life-altering break-up the last thing I had wanted to hear was that Sebastian thought I was on the prowl for a sugar daddy.

"I do actually need an assistant." He looked down, as though he was trying to gain composure and return to the previously professional tone of the evening.

"Well, that's your problem."

"You were perfect tonight. I saw the way you talked with the painters, so naturally. I need someone smart and sincere. I'm sorry I told you that I think you are drop-dead beautiful. It's the truth and it's better you know it. If you work for me, I promise I will keep my hands to myself. And I'll double what I was going to offer you."

I did need to make some money and socializing with artists on behalf of this rich guy seemed like a pretty easy thing to do. But I didn't want to be some kind of paid floozy.

I thought about what he'd said. Drop-dead beautiful. No one had ever called me that before. It was flattering in a strange way, and I believed that he wouldn't try anything. He looked so sincere. Anyway, I had to know what I was saying no to.

"What were you going to offer?"

"Three thousand a month plus an expense account for clothes and entertainment."

Holy shit. That was more than double what I made and I bought pretty much all my clothes at the Sally Ann.

"But, since my inappropriate confession, I understand that I've created an awkward working situation for you, so let's say six grand per month with a two thousand dollar expense allowance."

There were whole years when I lived on that amount. Well, practically. Back in my undergraduate days, I'd had six roommates and had eaten lentils for every meal. This was not the kind of job offer I was used to getting.

I looked at him while I mulled it all over in my head. I only needed to work for a couple of months on this salary to be able to set myself up in a new place. Besides, I had zero job prospects as a professor and it would take a while to get my applications out to various departments. It was basically this offer or the burger joint.

"Deal," the word came out of my mouth almost involuntarily.

We shook hands.

"I *am* terrible around beautiful women, I swear. Everything came out wrong and I'm sorry I angered you and embarrassed myself. I'm a work in progress. But I know how to behave myself, and I promise I will."

"Strictly professional," I said, still holding onto his hand for what was now an inappropriately long time.

"Of course," he said.

Chapter Three

When I told Monique about the evening, she freaked out.

"What'd I say? Watch out for him."

"Um, well, I took the job"

"You what?"

"He offered me six grand a month and another two grand for clothes and stuff."

"Oh my God. He wants you to be his mistress."

Why was there part of me that reveled in the idea? I had to wonder. But more importantly, I had to deny it. I was definitely going to take the job. I wanted to get to know him better and I trusted myself to not do anything stupid — so as long as I stuck with those basic tenets, I was sure it would all be fine.

"He swore to me it was strictly business."

"And you believed him?" She was incredulous. Monique had a way of making any man seem suspicious. She was very dramatic when she wanted to be.

"Well, yeah. Scout's honor."

She just shook her head. "Look, the going rate for this kind of work for someone who has never done it before is, like, three thousand, with like maybe two thousand in expenses."

"He said he was planning on offering three but since he made it awkward, he doubled it."

"Dirty trick."

"I can handle it. I'll make it work. I mean, even if I only stick around for a month, I'll make enough to be out of your hair and in my own apartment in no time."

She hugged me. "Claudia, you are not in my way. I love having you here."

I knew I eventually had to stand on my own again, though, and this was an opportunity that I didn't want to refuse. If I lasted even three weeks, I'd make enough to start the next chapter of my life. Until then, I had my emergency credit card.

Changing the topic, I said, "Hey, I need a new wardrobe to go with my new job. Let's go shopping."

* * * *

After a fairly unproductive trip to the mall—I didn't like shopping as much as I had when I was younger—Monique took me out for lunch. I rarely used to let her do this because I couldn't return the favor, but this time I knew money was coming and that I'd be able to treat her soon.

At the sleek downtown charcuterie eatery, we had a starter of olives and antipasti. Without even asking whether I was into it or not, Monique ordered a bottle of wine.

"Seriously?" I asked when the server was out of earshot. "It's two in the afternoon."

"Oh, eff it," she said. "I'm on a bender. I hate men."

"What did Jerome do this time?"

"Completely ignored my text message."

"What did you say?"

"I asked him if he missed me."

"Hmm. Maybe that was a little forward of you."

"Well, duh. I made a fool of myself. I don't know what's wrong with him. It's like he just knows how to bring out the worst in me."

"Are you sure that's it?" I asked.

The wine came. I decided there was no place I'd rather be than in this restaurant, sharing a bottle of Bordeaux with my best friend in the middle of the afternoon.

"Well, what's your take?"

"I think this is hard on you because you're so used to getting what you want from guys and he's not playing the game you're familiar with."

"Huh?" Her face scrunched up like she didn't want my perspective but I knew she did.

"I think he's your first real challenge. You're this sexy cowgirl who can bronco bust any steer she wants but this guy is your Texas Longhorn, the ultimate conquest, and you can't seem to lasso him in."

She finally laughed. I sensed the tension melt off her for a second.

Still giggling, she said, "That's it. He's my Texas Longhorn."

"So you have to up your game. Switch up your technique. If you want him, you can get him."

"I can, can't I?" She looked like a hero about to embark on an epic adventure.

We ordered more appetizers and the conversation got flowing. After my second glass, my own tensions finally began to melt away. "I want to find myself again," I told Monique. "I feel like I constrained myself for five years. Maybe I did that so I could focus on my work. Maybe somewhere deep inside, I needed my personal life to be dull so that I could just throw myself into the thesis. Now that it's done, it's time to find myself again."

"What do you want?"

"Nothing. No strings, anyway. No commitment. No big relationship. I just want to explore again. Get back out there. Have fun."

"Are you sure?"

"What do you mean?"

"I mean, in all the years I've known you, you have never been a no-strings kind of girl."

"Yeah, well, maybe it's time to turn a new leaf."

"This wouldn't have anything to do with working for a handsome polyamorous millionaire, would it?"

I felt naked. Nobody knew me better than Monique. "Uh, nothing at all."

She just smirked. "Well, from what I heard he's into smart women and he has relationships, not one-night stands."

Oh phew. I was relieved to hear it and Monique knew that. "Okay, fine. I'm totally gaga for my boss." I shook my head. "I'm not proud of this, okay?"

She smiled. "I did some digging for you. He's a good guy." She reached into her bag and brought out a file folder. "Here," she said, giving it to me. "Pictures of him with his wife at public events and there's also a photo of his lover from years back."

"Oh my God. I love you," I said. I'd been so curious.

"There's more." She handed me a package with a bow on it.

I looked at her, surprised. Then I unwrapped the present. It was a book called The Ethical Slut.

"Welcome to the modern era," Monique said.

"I thought you were against this stuff."

"I'm against cheating. Poly isn't cheating. It's very honest and I think given everything you've been through that it could work for you right now."

"Really?"

She nodded. My mind raced. I wanted so badly to throw my arms around Sebastian, to explore him completely, yet it had felt so wrong.

Until now.

* * * *

On Monday morning, I showered and dressed in my perfect new work outfit. Monique had helped me pick out a few classic items, so I wore a gray pencil skirt with a white blouse. I put my hair in a bun, and checked myself out in the mirror to make sure I looked prim and proper. Secretly, I felt like I was wearing a naughty librarian costume and I loved it.

It was strange to show up for work at the Porter mansion. Before the other night, I'd never even been to the neighborhood. Monique said she'd drive me on her way to work because it was my first day. The truth was she never drove to work because parking was so expensive. She just wanted to check out where the Porters lived.

As we pulled into the long driveway, she said, "I think it's weird that you have to work out of their home. What's that about?"

"I don't know if I'll always be here. It's probably just today. He wants me to see his collection and get a feel for the family's contributions to the arts."

"It's fishy, Claudia."

"Stop being paranoid," I said. "You said yourself he's a good guy, remember?"

Of course, the weirdness had crossed my mind many times already. I said a silent prayer that my gut feelings about Sebastian were the right ones and that the other stuff was all misunderstanding. Monique had all kinds of gossip on all the men in her world. It was just like a Jane Austen novel except these days so many of the young women weren't interested in marrying the men, but working for them or taking over their positions. The corporate world was so far removed from my own.

Riddled with self-doubt, I got out of Monique's car and made my way up the steps to the Porter mansion. The doorman answered and greeted me gracefully.

"I'm Claudia Richards," I said. "Here to see Mr Porter."

"Right this way, Miss Richards." He ushered me in.

The entrance hall was straight out of the movies. I'd never been in a home like this. It seemed provincial to admire the place too much, so I tried to act cool and not fixate too much on the wall of greenery in front of me. I'd seen that once before, in a magazine. I wanted so badly to go up to the wall and touch it to see if the plants were real but I knew they were. The skylight above provided ample light and I was sure the Porters had the latest in environmentally friendly design. You could tell by the sleek modern minimalism of the place.

Sebastian emerged from behind the wall, also dressed for work in a suit and tie. As soon as I saw him, I wanted to bolt. How could I pretend not to be attracted to him? I became flushed in a way that a job would not elicit. It was definitely his influence, the sexy slightly graying hair, his demure posture, and the sweet smile with which he greeted me. It was strange to think of him waking up and dressing that way just to go downstairs and I wondered if maybe that was the fundamental difference between the haves and the have-nots.

"Claudia," he said formally, "won't you come this way? I'll give you a tour of the place."

The depth of his voice was so alluring. He had the sound of a mid-century movie star, a debonair quality men these days simply did not have. It was like hearing Gregory Peck speak. I admonished myself to stop objectifying my new boss. How embarrassing. I hoped he didn't pick up on my inappropriate attention to details.

From a distance, I saw a pedestal with a lamp illuminating a sculpture. It had the appearance of flames, almost like a campfire, but when we got closer, I could tell it was actually three wire figures swirling around each other.

"This sculpture is one that my wife, Deb, selected. It's by a friend of ours, actually, a Spanish artist named Hatia D'Acosta."

"Ooh. It's intense."

"Oh, yes." He smiled. "Deb is actually in Spain visiting her right now."

"Oh?" I wanted to hear about his wife but I also didn't. Could it be any more obvious I had a huge crush on my new boss? "Is she considering another piece by the same artist?"

"I doubt that. We have three pieces by her already."

"Oh my. You must love her work."

"We love her. She's been a close family friend for many years. And, yes, her work is impressive."

We walked around the house that seemed to go on forever and ever. The entrée of the Porter mansion was more impressive than a hotel lobby, as though they had hired a designer to create a space in which the Porters could throw massive parties, Jay Gatsby style. I wondered how they could live here. But there was also an entire wing—the wing Sebastian said he lived in—that he didn't show me. I was curious, but of course I didn't dare ask. That would be flirting with disaster. Instead, I made clever comments on all of the formidable pieces of art—and he did have quite the collection. There were a lot of big names but there were also many pieces by relatively unknown artists, ones he told me he had met or studied with.

Then he pointed to a closed door and said, "And there's where I used to have my art studio. Now it's basically an expensive storage room."

His sardonic tone made me curious. "Can I see it?"

He paused and looked into my eyes, and I couldn't tell if he was flattered that I'd asked or disturbed.

"Why would you want to see a bunch of failed art?" he finally asked.

His humility was baffling. I was shocked that he could make self-deprecating comments. He had a veneer of success that made disparaging remarks seem completely out of place, and I couldn't help but observe his vulnerability and wonder how many others he'd shown it to. It certainly had not been apparent those other times I'd seen him out in the world being the big man everyone expected of him. The complexity of his situation coupled with the heated tension that I could feel between us made me dizzy.

"Commercial success means nothing," I replied.

"My paintings are failures on every level—commercially, technique wise, everything."

"Surely you're exaggerating. I think every good artist is self-critical." I wanted to let it go, continue the tour of the mansion and just leave Sebastian alone. For whatever reason, I couldn't help but be persistent. I was so curious.

"Fine, Claudia," he said as he opened the door.

There was still an easel poised in the middle of the room with the sun shining in on the hardwood floor. I walked in. He followed. Leaned against the wall were stacks of very large canvases, all square, maybe seven foot by seven foot in size. The ones facing forward were of faces, somewhat distorted and dark. Others were of women's figures, sort of grotesque.

"Intense," I muttered, aware suddenly of just how intimate a gesture it was for him to show me this room. "And solemn."

"Failure has that effect," he said.

"I don't think you should say that about them," I argued. "They are a form of expression. You shouldn't judge them so harshly."

"You don't hate them?"

"Not at all. I think they are deep and brooding and there is something ominous about them, but they are very expressive. I might even say passionate."

"Oh?" The tone of his voice was lighter, like he was relieved that I didn't feel the same way about them that he did.

I felt for him. I was deeply affected by his self-criticism, something I recognized from my own tendency to berate my work. Had I not also written and deleted and rewritten and deleted my own thesis about ten times because I hated the words that came out of me? It was intense to witness that quality in another. My peers had told me my thesis defense was brilliant, yet I could barely even recall a minute of it.

Creating art, much like creating an academic thesis is terribly lonely and I longed to tell Sebastian that I saw the value in his work.

"Yes. Sincerely."

"Well if this isn't the old cliché, I don't know what is."

"What do you mean?"

"My beautiful employee complimenting my art. You have no idea what that does for a wash-up like me."

I couldn't understand how he could refer to himself like that. "But you're the epitome of success," I retorted.

"Why? Because I was born into money? Please."

And there I had it. He'd laid out the paradox of his existence for me, and I finally understood what most people who grew up without much money didn't comprehend. In my childhood, lacking money was the biggest challenge. In his, I could see so clearly that wealth had been a burden. No wonder he took pleasure in giving it away.

"Well, that and your choice to support art instead of, I don't know, investing in oil drilling or something."

"Money means nothing to me and the more of it I give away, the better I feel."

"That's an impressive attitude," I said, feeling truly sympathetic. Not that I'd know what kinds of attitudes other rich people had, but I did think that Sebastian was generous.

I turned back to his work and admired the paintings one by one. In the silence of his studio, I felt the magnetic attraction between us. He stood behind me, just an inch too close. Was it purposeful? He'd called me beautiful again. It was hard to focus on the art in front of me.

There was a light knock on the door and a woman, presumably his housekeeper, entered. She was in her fifties, plump and maternal in her appearance. She wore a floral print smock.

"Oh, I'm sorry I interrupted," she said with a Scandinavian accent and began to close the door again.

"No, no," Sebastian said, a little too adamantly, like he was trying to cover up that maybe she had, in fact, interrupted. "What can I do for you?"

"Oh, I just wanted to know if you'd be here for lunch."

"Actually, Anne Lise, this is Claudia. She'll be working with us to distribute funds in the arts. She's going to be around now and then and I was thinking that since it's her first day, I'm going to make a good impression and take her out to lunch."

Anne Lise shook my hand and gave me a look that I couldn't quite detect, though it seemed like slight disapproval. Or maybe I was just feeling guilty because I had half been hoping my new boss would stand a little closer to me and kiss the back of my neck and she'd caught me.

I knew from that moment on that I was doomed. I wanted something to happen. This was not good.

* * * *

For lunch he took me to Le Papillon, a place I'd never even looked into all the times I'd walked by. It was in the St. Lawrence Market and had a reputation for being one of Toronto's best crêperies.

"You should try the Dos de Cod," he said. "The Matelot sauce is divine."

I didn't know what it was so I acquiesced and tried my best to feel as though I belonged. The server came, and Sebastian ordered two glasses of pinot grigio.

"I don't normally drink at lunch," I told him quietly, not wanting him to think I was unprofessional.

"Neither do I, but we're celebrating."

"Well, all right," I said. "Let the good times roll." I thought about the other day with Monique and silently resolved that I should sip slowly and drink lots of water.

The server laughed at my joke but Sebastian just smiled. "I don't expect you'll make a habit of it."

When the wine came, he raised his glass and said, "To the unfolding of a wonderful professional relationship. Thank you for taking a chance on us Porters."

"My pleasure," I said, clinking his glass.

I was nervous, as though we were out on a date. I found it very challenging to come up with professional lunch topics and wished I'd asked Monique for some advice. In the academic world, I might have run into one of the department heads or tenured professors in the cafeteria, but this was a completely different type of setting, one I only associated with girls' night out—when it was only Monique—or dates—but not dates I'd been on, just dates I'd heard about.

"Tell me a little more about yourself," Sebastian said. He took a sip from his glass.

"Well, let's see. I've dedicated my career to one long poem, so that's got to tell you something."

"Which poem?" he asked.

"*Paradise Lost* by Milton."

"Ah yes. *The mind is its own place and in itself can make a Heaven of Hell and a Hell of Heaven.*"

"You said you didn't know it," I blurted.

"I had good teachers at St. George's. Actually, I read it after you told me you were doing your PhD on him. He's dark. He engaged with the worst story in Western civilization. I can respect that."

"Yeah, that's what drew me to him," I said. "I'm into deep, dark and brooding."

Although I tried to make light of my career path, I wondered if he would think it a reference to the moment in his studio. Clearly he and Milton shared certain characteristics in that regard. I needed to change the topic.

"So do you and your wife travel much?" I asked. It seemed like an awkward question once I'd spoken it out loud.

"Ex-wife, actually. Well, we used to. She spends a good deal of time in Spain these days. Of course we try to take Sarah, our daughter, some place exotic at least once a year. I want her to see the world."

Did he say ex-wife? My mind replayed the words over and over. I tried to act cool. I fixated on the daughter part. "Oh, so how old is she? Your daughter?"

"Thirteen. She's at boarding school so you won't meet her around the house."

"Oh."

His world and mine seemed so different. I kicked myself for fantasizing about him. He was still an attached family man in the eyes of the world. There was no other way I could possibly interpret the ring and the fact that he and his wife — or *ex-wife* — still shared a home and went on vacations together. What was I doing? Yet, in my head, I did the math. He'd said he and his wife had been married for thirteen years. So had they got married because of a pregnancy? And if they were together for thirteen years, when had they separated? Oh, the drama. I wanted to know so much yet any more questioning on the matter would be totally inappropriate.

"So you teach at U of T?"

"I am a TA. I'm hoping to teach a course of my own someday but everything in the academic world takes time."

"Indeed." He nodded. After a pause, he said, "Well, you're young. You have time. Actually, if you don't mind my asking, how old are you?"

"Twenty-seven."

"A baby still. At your age, I'd barely figured anything out yet. Deb and I married young. We actually grew up together. We were childhood sweethearts."

"Wow," I gasped. "That is so sweet."

"Yes, very sweet." He smiled. "But we still had a lot of growing to do after marriage. I mean, we're still growing now. That's one of the things I appreciate most about Deb. She has a willingness to grow. Some people don't. They get stuck in roles, in relationships and they stop growing."

"I relate," I said, way too bluntly. How I wished I could keep my mouth shut.

"You? Impossible."

"No, I relate. Remember the caterer boyfriend I told you about the other night?"

"Yes, yes. The guy with the canapés. I wish I'd paid closer attention."

"Yeah. We were together for five years and I think I got kind of stuck, like what you're saying."

"Were you monogamous?"

"Well, yeah." I was surprised by his question. It seemed pretty obvious that we would be. "We were living together."

"Well, not all couples who live together are monogamous."

I didn't say anything.

"My wife and I had an open marriage for years," he finally said.

"Oh yeah?" I didn't know how to react to this. Was he serious? Was it a test to see if I was interested? I was a gigantic ball of confusion, trying desperately not to create uncomfortable undertones.

"We've practiced polyamory for almost the entire duration of our marriage."

"Really?" I was completely incredulous. But now Monique's gossip vine made a whole lot more sense. No wonder people talked about the Porters, especially if Sebastian was, technically, an eligible bachelor. "Did that ever create problems for you?" I asked then immediately regretted my stupidity. "Don't answer that. Forget I asked. I'm sorry. I can say idiotic things sometimes."

And the wine was not helping.

"It's fine. No, it never created problems. At least, not bigger problems than the alternative."

"I see," I said. "But you're divorced now?"

"As a matter of fact, yes. Almost. We're finalizing the paperwork soon, but we'll always be family."

"And you're still wearing your wedding ring."

"Yeah." He looked at his hand. "I like it. It was my great-grandfather's."

I needed a diversion, a different subject, anything to stop myself from asking all the inappropriate questions plaguing my mind. "So what's the best place you've ever traveled to?"

I was desperate to stop talking about their marriage and terrified that it showed. Like a real gentleman, Sebastian made sure we didn't discuss anything personal after that.

"Hmm," he mused. "I'm going to say Prague."

Chapter Four

A couple of weeks later, nothing had happened except the going-through of motions that suggested professionalism with a torturous attraction that was anything but professional. Of course, I said nothing and made sure never to bring up Deb or my personal life. Every time he came near me, I felt the heat of our connection. It was one thing to work remotely from home and make occasional trips to his house to do paperwork. The far greater challenge was in showing up to events with him.

We were in the back of his car headed for the airport for an overnight trip—our first. The destination was Calgary and the occasion was special to Sebastian because one of his previous art instructors was having an opening. It was a small affair at a coffee shop and gallery but Sebastian had funneled thousands of dollars into it.

"Major galleries could never be interested," he told me. "Malcolm's work is just way too advanced."

"I can't wait to see it," I said.

"I can't wait to see what you think of it."

"I'm sure I'll like it."

He shook his head. "Don't be too sure."

We flew first class, which was new for me. I got a bit tipsy from the bubbly and Sebastian had a limo waiting for us once we got our bags. Not long after that, we pulled into the Fairmont Palliser Hotel. Sebastian checked us in while I waited in the lobby. I had no idea anything so opulent existed in Calgary. When we got into the elevator, he pushed the top button.

As he gave me my room card, he said, "Drinks in the Gold Lounge in an hour? Then we can go from there."

"Yes. Sounds good."

Down the hall, I opened my door and almost peed my pants at the sight of the suite. It was twice as large as the apartment I'd shared with Pete. After looking around, I noticed I'd spent about fifteen minutes totally stupefied by the spectacular view and the king-sized bed. I stripped down then got into the shower, complete with jets from all sides and a huge showerhead.

I dressed in my new Bebe cocktail party dress that Monique helped me pick out. It had hues of purple and gray in silky soft fabric that made me feel so feminine. I paired it with some Fluevog heels and put my hair into a simple bun. Sebastian had complimented me on every outfit so far but I wanted to express my appreciation through fashion. This was the old me, the real me, coming out again. I tried something new that Monique and I had practiced at her place. Liquid liner. It was dramatic and I dare say, I looked good. When I examined myself in the mirror, I appeared to be a better version of me, and I realized, in that moment, that ever since Sebastian had come into my life, I had started to actualize my potential. I patted myself down and marveled at the reflection of the real me. It was time to meet Sebastian.

The hotel was so lovely that it took me a long time to get to the bar. I wanted to stop and admire the chandeliers and décor.

"Claudia, you are magnificent," he said when I walked into the Golden Lounge. He got off his chair and stood. He was a gentleman greeting a lady.

His manners were still foreign to me but I sure admired them.

"Are you enjoying your room?" he asked.

"Oh my God, I want to move in," I said.

He laughed.

I saddled up on the barstool beside him. "So what kind of drink goes with my dress tonight, Mr Porter?"

"A dress like that should not be upstaged. I suggest a clear beverage, perhaps a vodka martini or a gin and tonic."

When the bartender came, I ordered a plain soda. I was already drunk on Sebastian's compliments. I didn't need to add anything else to the mix.

* * * *

At the gallery, I understood right away why Sebastian had been unsure. Malcolm's paintings depicted various group sex positions. Each one was unapologetically erotic and full of erections and women with orgasm faces. It was overwhelming. The spectators all knew what they were there to see so there were a lot of fishnets and red lipstick in the crowd.

"I always thought Calgary was a pretty conservative city," I whispered.

"It is. Conservative cities always have the best seedy underbellies," he said. "That's why Malcolm thrives here."

Sebastian, being a man of good breeding, did not acknowledge the sexual nature of the paintings and talked instead about their composition and Malcolm's technique. It killed me. Did he have any idea how he was torturing me?

Malcolm got up and said his welcome then talked about the inspiration for the paintings, which was supposedly not sex but Simone de Beauvoir. It sounded to me like he was full of it but I didn't care. All I could think about was Sebastian beside me, the pull between us, how he was standing even closer than usual.

"I'd like to thank one of Canada's most important members of the art community, Sebastian Porter, for sponsoring this event," Malcolm said, putting his hands together so the crowd would follow suit and applaud.

All eyes were on us and Sebastian did something unexpected. He looped his arm in mine and bowed slightly in acknowledgment of the crowd. I was so taken aback. Why had he done that?

Later on, we circulated and mingled, and I studied the paintings more closely.

Suddenly, Sebastian was behind me. His breath tickled my neck when he whispered, "Which one is your favorite?"

"This one," I said, not turning around. Instead, I fixated on the painting, by all accounts, a pornographic image of a woman in the throes of passion with two men at her disposal.

"What do you like about it?"

I couldn't believe what he was asking. If I told him the truth, I'd die of embarrassment.

"The colors, of course," I said.

"I see."

There was an awkward silence as we stood there staring at a painting of a woman sandwiched between two men, one of whom was penetrating her vaginally, the other of whom was penetrating her anally. After a long silence, I had to say something.

"It's the expression on her face that gets to me."

"Oh?"

"Well, yeah. Look at the pleasure she's taking in this."

"You don't think she'd be in pain?" he asked, seeming concerned for her.

"Only the best kind of pain," I said, perhaps a little too quickly.

Sebastian leaned in close and whispered in my ear, "You're killing me, Claudia. You know that, don't you?"

I turned, and looked at him, and feigned total innocence. "I have no idea what you are talking about, Mr Porter."

"I don't believe you," he said. "You know very well what you are doing."

I stepped just one more centimeter into his personal space so that our bodies were almost touching. This prompted more whispering.

"Do you have any idea how sexy you are?"

Again, I feigned innocence. "Me?"

"I'm overcome by desire, Claudia."

"Oh really," I said. "Maybe we should get some wine and sit down." Then a pang of doubt came on. What was I doing with this married man? Who had I become?

He gulped. "Yes. Definitely."

He fetched drinks for us while I took a seat. My panties were entirely soaked from the delicious torture I'd put him through. Maybe he didn't know it went both ways. Poor Sebastian, he could be such a clueless man that way.

We sat down on a cozy dark burgundy couch in the corner.

"Thank you for offering me this position," I said as a way to break the awkward silence. "I'm enjoying spending time with you."

"The pleasure is all mine," he said.

I gave him my most coy look. "Mmmm. Pleasure is right."

"Claudia, you have to stop torturing me."

"Do I?"

"No." He shook his head. "Please continue."

"I thought so," I said. "So tell me. What do you think of my favorite painting?"

"Well—" He cleared his throat. "I think it is highly erotic and I can't quite imagine what a good girl like you sees when she looks at it."

"Possibility," I said. "After all, life imitates art."

"Does it now?"

"It most certainly can."

"Claudia," he said, fixating on my legs as though he couldn't fathom the idea of making eye contact with me at that moment. "I have developed a massive and extremely unprofessional crush on you. I think you are the most seductive and enticing woman I have ever known."

His confession seemed sincere, and for a second, I felt a pang of compassion for him, reminded suddenly of the complexity of his being, aware of how genuine he sounded. I wondered what it was like to be in an even longer partnership than what I'd experienced with Pete and what it had been like for him to share his wife with other partners. I wanted so badly to know more about him and the circumstances of his marriage but I was also afraid to find out. I was so smitten with him.

I watched him, wanting to catch his eyes but he was still looking down.

"You have no idea how much I long to be with you," he continued. "It's all I can think about lately. Deborah knows. She knows me very well. I keep no secrets from her."

She knows about me? And he called her Deborah, not Deb. Was it possible he was distancing himself from her, or was I reading too much into his something so subtle? "Um, excuse me?"

"Yeah, she and I have no secrets between us, especially where attraction to others is concerned."

This was news. "Oh?"

"She's in Spain right now with her lover," he continued. "I need your assurance that this will stay between you and me. You see, our family is very wrapped up in maintaining our privacy, especially for Sarah's sake."

"You can trust me," I said and meant it.

"My wife is bisexual," he said. "She knew it when we first got together but she was not able to tell her family and risk her inheritance. You remember the sculptures in our home?"

"Yes."

"They were all made by her lover."

"Oh."

"Actually, that one in the foyer is inspired by the three of us. Our relationship."

"So do you and…Hatia…?"

"No, no, not like that. Hatia is Deb's lover, not mine. But I do consider her family. I love her very much and have a lot of respect for her art and for her as a human being."

This was one of the strangest conversations I'd ever had. I understood the words he spoke but I didn't completely comprehend the meaning behind them.

"So hold on. Did you say that Deb's parents would take away her inheritance for being bisexual?" I blurted. What kind of people would do that?

"Not exactly. They aren't bigots. But they are traditional. She was supposed to marry well and have perfect children. And so was I. We did all that. In some ways, we had the best marriage I know of. We are still very honest with each other but these days we are better off living separate lives even though we share a home when she's not in Spain."

"What does Sarah think of your arrangements?"

"She doesn't know. She's at boarding school and it's hard for her. I don't think that teenagers want to know too much about their parents' intimate relations anyway so Deborah and I have kept it very quiet."

"So you're keeping your divorce a secret?"

"For now. We're adjusting to it ourselves before we share the news with others."

"I see," I said, trying to take it all in. "So how does she know about me, then? How did I come up in conversation?"

"Like I said, we don't have any secrets from each other. We always had a rule about disclosing all potential lovers so there were no surprises. It's out of respect for each other."

"So you think of us as potential lovers?"

"No, Claudia. I don't. I know I don't stand a chance with a gorgeous woman such as you but I did tell Deborah that I'm attracted to you."

"You did?"

He nodded. "Ever since that day at the fundraiser when I saw you in your pink dress and you lit up the room, I've been smitten with you."

"So this job offer was just a ploy to get in my pants?" I asked, again a little too quickly, but my emotions were out of control.

"No, no," he said. "I did need someone. I was in a bind and I knew you were competent, and you are and I'm still not trying to *get into your pants*, as you put it."

"You're not?"

"I swore to you that I wouldn't."

"Too bad," I said.

"Too bad?" He looked at me in disbelief.

"Sebastian, it's mutual. I'm totally attracted to you. I've been fighting it because you're my boss and you're married or semi-married and I have a lot of respect for the institution of marriage. I've been cheated on and it hurts like hell, and I vowed never to engage in anything like that."

"Oh, Claudia. What kind of moron would cheat on you?" He shook his head. "I'm so sorry that happened to you. You deserve so much better."

"The caterer."

"I wish I'd known. I'd have complained."

"I wasn't going to tell you about the cheating. I vowed I never would. I didn't want you to think less of me."

"Why would I think less of you?"

"For choosing a guy like that, for having low standards." Suddenly my eyes welled up, and I couldn't fight back the tears. "I cared what you thought of me. I tried to tell myself I didn't but I did. I wanted you to like me."

"Oh, Claudia, I like you so much it hurts."

"Really?"

"Really."

He took my hands in his and looked deep into my eyes, and I thought I was going to melt. His gaze was so hot and intense.

"Claudia, you are precious and you deserve to be treated well."

"Pete — that's his name — was my first real boyfriend. Like I mentioned, we lived together for five years. In fact, we were still living together on the night of the pink dress. Actually, that was the night I caught him. I walked in on him. It was in our bed."

"Oh, Claudia." He pulled me to him and even though we were sitting side-by-side next to each other, we kind of hugged like that.

I rested my head on his shoulder. He smelled divine. Tears rolled down my cheek and it was cathartic to finally tell him the truth about myself.

He sat back, reached into the inside pocket of his suit jacket and took out a handkerchief and offered it to me. I dried my eyes.

"When you offered me the job, I needed the money so I took it. I told Pete to move out of our apartment that very night and I was never able to go back there. Monique was awesome. She paid for movers to put my stuff in boxes and bring everything to her storage space."

He listened patiently and shook his head.

"My life is in shambles right now, to tell the truth. The only good thing I've got going on is you."

"Claudia, you have no idea what it means for me to hear this."

"It doesn't change your opinion of me?"

"Only for the better," he said. "I can help. Let me help you find an apartment."

"I was afraid of that," I said. "Look, it's nice of you to offer, but I'm not into being a kept woman if that's what you're getting at. I've got my sights set higher. I want to be a professor and a scholar. I want to take care of myself. I'm not interested in having a man bail me out. Besides, I'm pretty messed up over Pete. I'm not sure I can put myself in a vulnerable situation with a man again for a long time. And I need to solve my own problems."

"You misunderstood me. I didn't mean to imply I'd solve your problems. It sounds to me like you're doing a good job of doing that yourself. I'm glad you moved in with Monique instead of staying in the old apartment."

"You are?"

"Of course. It shows a lot of self-respect. But I'd be happy to help you find an apartment of your own. And if it's a matter of money, just say the word and I'll handle it."

"No, that's what I mean. I have to do it on my own."

"Okay. I understand. Deborah is also independent. I'm used to that, just so you know. I expect nothing less of the women in my life. Even Sarah has her own savings and doesn't ask me for anything."

Suddenly the intimacy of our conversation dawned on me and I remembered that we were at a highly publicized art event. There were photographers standing about and I didn't want to have this moment captured for the gossip columns.

"Oh my God, it's totally unprofessional of me to be sitting here pouring out my feelings and problems to my boss in the middle of an important evening."

"There's nothing I'd rather have from you than honesty," Sebastian said. "Besides, we've made our appearance and we're free to go. Malcolm has his entourage now. Let's continue this conversation back at the hotel."

"I'd like that," I said.

He looped my arm in his and led me out of the café. And the feeling that I could trust him and that he cared about me only augmented my desire. During the ride home I tried to digest all the new information I'd received. I was shocked that his marriage was the way he said it was. I'd heard about such arrangements but I never imagined I'd meet someone with that kind of set-up.

"Would you care to join me in my room for a nightcap?" Sebastian asked.

"Splendid," I said.

Although, now that our feelings were out in the open, I was apprehensive. It might not have been the brightest idea to move forward, especially considering I didn't want to interfere in his family life and I was pretty sure I still had growing to do before getting involved in another relationship. Maybe by poly, he meant he slept around a lot and if that were the case, I'd swap one awful situation for another. What was I doing? And why did it feel so right to spend time with him?

We entered his suite and it was even more stunning than my own. I could not believe it. There was a huge open space and off to the side there was the beginning of a living room space. The view of the city was great, even though Calgary was flat and the buildings within view were all fairly low to the ground. That said, the lights glimmered and gave the impression of vastness and possibility.

I could barely stand being in the vicinity of Sebastian without flirting with him. As he uncorked a bottle of sparkling wine and poured two flutes, I sat on the leather couch and waited for him, wondering what it would be like to throw caution to the wind and make love to him the way I wanted. Would he think I was too forward? Would he still respect me?

"Sebastian, can I ask you something?"

"Anything."

"If I'd said yes to being spoiled by you that night after the first party we attended together, what would have happened?"

"Well," he said, "I'd have jumped at the opportunity to take you out for some lovely experiences and buy you a few pretty things, but I'm glad you said no, because if you hadn't, you wouldn't be here with me now."

"True."

"And I'm glad you're here with me right now."

Something was still bugging me, though, and I decided I better clear the air before going any further. "So you love to spoil women with things, is that right?"

"I've been known to take pleasure in sharing my wealth, yes."

"So if you see some hot knockout downstairs in the lobby tomorrow, you might approach her with the same offer you offered me?"

"Ah," he said as though it just occurred to him what I meant. "I get it. You want to know if I hit on women. Well, the answer is no. I was completely taken by you. I handled it wrong, and I'm sorry, but I want you to know that I would never try to buy your affection or anyone else's. That's the one thing about growing up with money. You learn to figure out pretty quickly who sees you for you and who only sees you as a provider. I knew that night, after I made an idiot out of myself and embarrassed you, that you are the kind of person who can see other people clearly."

I gazed at the view.

He sat down next to me and handed me a glass. "To your beauty," he said.

We clinked flutes and I took a sip, feeling the rush of bubbles on my palate.

"Sebastian?"

"Yes," he answered.

"What would you do if I kissed you?"

He appeared to be surprised. "Um, well, I'd like that very much," he said.

I put my glass down on the side table then took his from him and placed it beside mine. Then, still clad in my heels, I straddled him, my knees touching the back of the couch, as I rested on his lap. Seductively, I leaned in. My lips met his and we shared a delicious slow and sensual kiss. I wanted him so badly, and it was clear from the hardness in his pants that he wanted me too. We kissed for a long time. It was soft and romantic, satisfying a yearning we'd both been feeling for a long time now. I stroked his chest then lowered my hand until it was upon his hardness. I moaned at his reaction to my touch.

"Sebastian, you are so sexy. Do you know that?"

"Oh, Claudia, you have no idea what it's like hearing you say this."

"I want to explore you all over," I purred.

"You're so beautiful."

"I have wanted you since that first night. Something about you mystified me and captured my imagination. I've been fantasizing about you ever since."

He traced the neckline of my dress. He caressed my skin and ran his fingers along my neck. It tingled everywhere and it was like being massaged even though the touch was so light. He cupped the back of my neck with his palm.

"I want to kiss you again," he whispered, pulling me in.

Our lips locked once more. For an instant, it felt so deliciously wrong, like I was a complete and utter tart, a real strumpet. I played out the fantasy of being a bad girl instead of the good girl I'd been my whole life. Perhaps that's why I remembered Sebastian's agreement with Deb and wondered whether I could trust it to be true. What had Monique meant about him having a reputation? In spite of my own desire for him, I held back.

"Is something wrong?" he asked.

"Just…"

"What is it, Claudia?"

"I'm haunted by something."

"What's troubling you?"

I reached for his left hand and lifted it up to show him.

"This," I said, pointing to his wedding ring.

"I told you. It's complicated. The divorce papers are almost done. Deborah is in Spain and she has given me her blessing."

"But…" I tore myself away from him completely and sat down beside him, newly sober from thinking of myself as a harlot and seeing myself in a way that I never had before. "I don't know where I fit into your arrangement."

"Well, where would you like to fit in?"

"How many women have you slept with besides your wife?" Even as the words left my mouth, I regretted them. I sounded so judgmental and paranoid but suddenly I was.

"Claudia." He looked into my eyes. "Where is this coming from?"

"I don't know." I could feel tears welling, and I prayed that he couldn't see them. Why was I suddenly so emotional? "I've never been 'the other woman'."

"Oh." He rested his palm on my shoulder in an avuncular way.

The mood was gone, replaced by two confused, still slightly aroused people forced into a relationship conversation. Part of me wanted to forget it, throw caution to the wind and explore his erection again. The sane part of me knew that if I did, this would end horribly and I'd never forgive myself.

"I'm probably not what you think," I said. "I've only had one boyfriend. That is, one sexual partner. I'm not some kind of floozy and I don't want to get strung along in some complicated soul-demeaning type of affair."

"Claudia, I would never think of you as a floozy. You are a PhD candidate, for crying out loud. You're way smarter than me and most of the people I know."

"Then why do I feel like I'm doing something dumb?" The tears threatened to overflow.

"I think that's my fault. I have nothing but the highest respect for you."

"It's a little hard for me to believe, you know."

"Why?"

"Because I've never known anyone like you before. I don't know anyone who's polyamorous marriage is coming to an end, who still wears his wedding ring and in all likelihood will continue to because he likes the way it looks. You're very confusing to me."

"Ah, so you don't have much experience with complicated situations."

"None. Zip. Zilch."

"Well, I apologize. I should be taking it much more slowly. I got all wrapped up in tonight. But you're right. It would be better for you to meet Deb and Hatia first and we can all discuss it together."

Now, that was just weird to me. "What?"

"Well, I assume you want to meet them. Am I wrong?"

"Sebastian, this sounds awfully complicated. I'm just a girl with a crush and I feel like I'm out of my league here."

"I'm the one who is out of my league."

"I'm not sure I have what it takes to be in this kind of relationship. I mean, frankly, I don't even know if you want a relationship. I don't know if you're still sleeping with Deb. Or other girls. Maybe this is a sex only thing for you and if so I'm so embarrassed that I admitted my feelings for you." I was mortified by myself, actually. I got up to leave. Time to go back to my suite. This was enough torture for me. "Listen, I'm sorry if I'm confusing you and I'm sorry if I led you on. This probably isn't for me. I don't know if you want me to quit or what but maybe we can discuss it back in Toronto."

"Claudia, don't go. I'm the one who should apologize. I have done a terrible job of communicating. So let's take a step back. First of all, Deb and I haven't slept together in a long time. Years. Second, there is nobody else."

I sighed a sigh of relief and felt myself settle down. "Okay, well that's good to know. I was scared that I was just one in a crowd."

"I never meant to scare you. I've longed to be in love again and…"

In love? Did he just say that? "What?"

"I mean, I…" He looked down sheepishly, like he had said too much.

"Did you say love?" I pestered. I had to know.

"Well, I have feelings for you, Claudia. Strong feelings. That's why I should not have arranged this trip. I didn't know we would flirt the way we did. I didn't realize we might end up in this…situation. Frankly, I didn't think you would ever go for an old man like me."

"Stop saying that. You're not old."

"Then you're young."

"I'm not that young," I protested. "There is a perfectly reasonable and respectable age difference between us. What gets me is that you're still semi-married and I have no intention of being a mistress."

"You wouldn't be a mistress. Hatia is not a mistress."

"Well, what is she then?"

"A friend of the family," he said in all seriousness. Then he smiled and said, "A rather good friend."

"So is that what you want from me? My friendship?"

He nodded. "And your understanding, and companionship, and your stunningly beautiful mouth." He stared at my mouth longingly and ran his thumb across my bottom lip. "You have no idea how sexy your pout is."

"Quit changing the topic," I said because it was turning me on to have him look at me like that, and I didn't know what to do with my own arousal.

"Claudia, what can I do to put you at ease?"

"Well, you can answer my question about your other lovers."

"In all of the nearly twenty-five years of marriage, there have been three," he told me. "But that includes you."

"Then why have I heard you have a reputation?"

"Who said that?"

"Never mind."

"Was it Monique?"

"No." I would never admit that. What was he thinking? "Just answer the question."

"Well, the last relationship didn't end all that well. I was maligned."

"Oh, I see. So it was her fault that you got a reputation."

"That's not what I meant. Don't put words in my mouth." His face became stern. "She wanted money. She threatened us and she went to the tabloids with all kinds of gossip. In the end, she admitted that she was emotionally unstable and actually she is currently on pretty heavy prescription medications."

"You're still in touch with her?"

"Sure. She's not an enemy. She just had a rough patch."

"Oh. Sorry," I said, aware of how judgmental I'd sounded. "What about the other one?"

"Well, that was Hatia. And it was just a one-time thing for me."

"What?"

"Yeah. Deb and I met her together. We had this mistaken and terrible idea that having a threesome would somehow improve the spark between us. It did improve the sparks in her life but not so much in mine. It was easily the most ego-damaging experience of my life, being in bed with two lesbians."

"I thought you said she was bisexual."

"She seemed like a lesbian that night, that's for sure."

It wasn't funny, but I couldn't help but laugh. "Your ego took a beating, did it?"

"You can say that again. I don't want to get into details but I couldn't even think about getting physical with women again for a while."

"But isn't it painful for you that they're together now?" I pictured his paintings again. The women in them seemed ugly, almost deformed, as though the painter himself had been rejected by them. The puzzle started to come together.

"Not at all. I genuinely like Hatia," he said and from his tone I could tell he meant it. "I have a lot in common with her, though apparently she's a better lover than me."

I laughed awkwardly. "I'm sorry. It's not funny." I shook my head, looked out of the window again at the view that seemed much more pleasant than it had just a few minutes prior.

"Please. Go ahead. We have to be able to laugh at ourselves. Wouldn't you agree?"

"Yes. So when was that?"

"The awful threesome? That was on our trip to Spain some eleven years ago now."

"Wow, that long ago?"

"Yeah."

"And the troubled woman?"

"Nadia. That was two years ago. Like I said, it didn't last very long. I didn't know her all that well. I obviously wouldn't have gotten involved if I did."

"You seem pretty confident that I'm not crazy."

"Are you crazy?"

"No."

"See?" He was so handsome when he smiled.

"Honestly, I feel a lot better now that I know about your past. For some reason, when you said you were polyamorous, I had the impression you slept with a ton of women, and maybe I'm just insecure but I wasn't sure how to make sense of it."

"Maybe you don't have a lot of respect for men after what happened with Pete."

"I was hurt by that."

"Relationships are hard. Anyone who has been married for as long as I have knows that marriage is all about honesty and compromise. When Deb recognized that she was more attracted to Hatia than me, it hurt but we got through it, and not just because it was expected. I still love her dearly. She's a great mother and she's always been honest with me."

"You seem very mature in the way you're handling it," I said, feeling totally inexperienced compared to him. "Or maybe I am kind of young,"

"That's precisely why I shouldn't rush things with you. I like you. There you have it. It's the honest truth. I feel something between us I've never felt before and I can imagine falling completely and madly in love with you. So I don't want to rush. I want you to meet Deb and Hatia and my daughter, if you want."

I could not believe that he was handing me everything—his past and his present—on a silver platter like this. It was hard for me to understand what to make of this. I mean, he was so honest, so sincere and I loved spending time with him.

"Really?" I was overcome with shyness in that moment.

He took my hand in his. "I don't know how else to get you to believe that I am deeply, deeply moved that you kissed me tonight and I don't want to put us at risk."

"Us? Are we an 'us'?"

"You tell me. I'll let you sleep on it. I think you better go to your suite now. We have an early flight."

"But..."

"But what?" he asked so seductively, gazing into my eyes. He looked so intense, so overwhelmingly hot.

I leaned in to try to kiss him but he pulled away.

"I learned something very important tonight," he said. "I learned that you might actually have it in you to consider being with me and I don't want to risk that for anything. We are going to move very slowly, Claudia. I don't want you to think I'm only interested in having some kind of fling with you."

"So no goodnight kiss?" I batted my lashes at him.

"I'm afraid not."

He led me to the door. "I'll see you in the morning."

"Really?" I was shocked. "Not even one last kiss?"

"Really. Now stop acting like such a tart," he said playfully, spanking my bottom.

It wasn't hard or anything. In fact, the sensation filled me with ecstasy. I'd never been disciplined before and I liked it when he told me what to do or what not to do, as the case was. I locked eyes with him. Our gazes held us in a torturously chaste pose, like magnets.

"Goodnight, Sebastian" I finally managed.

"Goodnight, sweet Claudia. I will think of you as I fall asleep."

"Will you jerk off?" I asked. I was just being playful but his eyes told me that I was onto something.

"Do you want me to?"

"Yes," I whispered and touched his hardness one final time. I wanted nothing more than to fall to my knees and free him from the constraints of his clothing, take his hard dick in my mouth and blow his mind with my desire to please him, but naturally I couldn't do that and it was deeply, deeply frustrating.

He moaned into my ear, and I was so wet that I'd probably leave a mark if I sat down anywhere.

"Goodnight, Claudia. Sweet dreams. I will think of you when I come."

This was torture. But two could play at that game. I moaned, too, and touched the neckline of my dress while I bit my lower lip, all the while maintaining eye contact with him. "I'll be thinking of you while I touch myself, too," I said. Through my dress, I fingered my left nipple with my right hand. I moaned again and his eyes widened like he could not stand it. To say we wanted each other would have been the understatement of the century. I could barely tear myself away from his magnetic pull.

I went back to my room, my temporary palace, and dropped my drawers as soon as I got inside. I went straight to the bathroom and examined the tub. Thank God—there was a detachable showerhead. Of course there was.

It was golden and huge. Of course it was.

I took a towel off the heated rack and sat down with my feet in the tub as I filled it with hot water and ran some sudsy bubble bath under the tap. I had a look at myself in the mirror and I liked what I saw. Monique had been right before. I had become mousy with Pete. I'd forgotten myself. The real me was reemerging at full speed and she was sensual and sexy. She knew how to let her hair down and get what she wanted. And sure, tonight hadn't gone perfectly. I'd got a little too dramatic about Sebastian's situation, but I forgave myself for it because it was hard to trust a man when I'd just been hurt by another one. As weird as it all was, there was something about this that I could trust. Life was full of surprises.

I got an idea. I stepped out, dried my feet on the bath mat then went for my phone, which was strewn along with my clothes in a line from the bathroom to the entrance of the suite. I picked it up and brought it back with me. I dialed Sebastian's suite as I pulled the lever above the tap so that the warm water spurted out of the showerhead instead.

I heard him answer but I didn't say anything. Instead, I put the phone on speaker and set it out of harm's way then got comfortable on the ledge of the tub, seated on the warm towel. I moaned as I ran the hot water over my thighs. My skin was so receptive to the warmth. I touched my wetness and that's when I completely let myself go. I nearly forgot the phone was even there as I used the showerhead and the weight of the water streaming down on my pussy to turn myself on. With my left hand I fondled my breasts and gave each nipple a tug and squeeze as I imagined Sebastian in the room with me and what it would feel like to have his mouth create these delicious sensations for me.

It occurred to me to set the showerhead to the massage function and when I did, Sebastian told me he liked it. "Yeah, baby," were his precise words. I moaned again and so did he. The pulsating water throbbed against my clit and sent me into wild ecstasy. I couldn't help but let myself get a little louder, especially since I could tell it was turning him on. And who had I become? Where had this femme fatale been hiding all these years? I didn't care where it was coming from. I welcomed it. I wanted nothing more than to be his fantasy. It got me so hot thinking about him thinking about me. Nothing but these opulent and tastefully decorated walls between us. How perfect. Soon I heard him join me.

"Mmmm. Yeah," I said. "I wanna hear you come."

He emitted a sexy moan.

"I want to fuck you, Claudia. I want it so bad it's taking everything to not burst through those doors, lay you down and fuck you so hard you'll never forget it."

I moaned. "I'm going to make you come so hard."

"You already are."

"Are you coming?" By the time I asked, I already knew the answer. It was so loud, so satisfying to listen to. I felt like I was right there with him. In a sense, I was.

"Let me hear you, baby."

His order delighted me.

It was so weird how that word affected me. I'd hated it the one and only time Pete had called me that. Yet now, with Sebastian's voice forming the word, it sounded so sexy, so perfect. Baby. I was his sexy plaything. I moaned and the water beat down on my clit as I thought about him licking my pussy. I couldn't wait for that. Nothing could make me come harder than oral sex, just the right speed and pressure and I was sure Sebastian was someone who knew what to do. I could just tell. The thought of it—of the delights to come—sent me over the edge and I cried out in ecstasy. My orgasm was so strong. I sighed as I turned off the water and slipped, limply, into the tub. I was wrapped in the velvet of sudsy, sweet-scented water.

"Mmm. That was so good," I purred.

"It'll be better when we're together. Believe me. I'll give you orgasms you never even knew you could have." His voice was like melted chocolate with whipped cream.

"I believe you," I said. "I can't wait."

"Claudia, I can't believe what a vixen you are."

Suddenly, I was self-aware and no longer a total vixen. "Oh, stop."

Orgasm always did that to me. Once I came, it was all over. The illusion of sexiness, the feeling of intimacy. I went back to being my regular old self. But this time was different because my regular self was still in the most decadent hotel room of her life, in a sultry bath with a sexy man on the phone beside her. I was kind of relieved that Sebastian wasn't there because a tear forced its way out of my eye. I had no control over it and I wasn't sad. It was just that for the first time in my life, I still felt sexy after coming.

"It's true," Sebastian said, as though he could read my mind. "You are the most gorgeous and sexy woman I have ever known."

I didn't say anything because more tears started to flow.

"Claudia?"

"Yeah?"

"Why are you so quiet?"

"I don't know."

"Can I come over?"

"I thought you wanted us to wait."

"I do. Get dressed."

"All right."

We hung up, and I stepped out of the tub and toweled off using another towel right from the heat rack. These heated towels were a real luxury. Still naked, I walked out into the bedroom and went to my suitcase. I took out my satin pajama pants and tank top. Why had I packed this if not for some subconscious conviction that Sebastian would see it? And now I was so glad.

There was a faint knock at my door. I pulled the tank over my head and put on each leg of the pants as I fumbled toward the door. Maybe I had seductive moments but I was also a bit of a klutz. When I opened the door, Sebastian grabbed me and held me in his arms in a strong embrace. That pushed me over the edge in a different way and my tears flowed easily. Instead of fighting them, I just let them come. I had needed to purge these tears for a while. I hadn't even let myself cry over Pete or the loss of my apartment, a place I called home for four years. Finally I was in Sebastian's arms where I felt safe.

"Come in," I whispered.

"Claudia, you're crying." He examined my face and wiped my tears away with his thumb. He cupped me beneath my right ear. "Why are you crying?"

"I—I just get emotional sometimes, especially after sex, not that we had sex but—" I started to explain.

"You're so beautiful. Your tears don't scare me." His eyes were so warm. "Can I get you anything?"

"No."

"Can I take you to your bed?"

"Yes."

I loved how he took control of the situation, how he knew exactly what I needed. All I wanted was to be in his arms. At the bed, he pulled back the covers, propped up the pillows and got in. I noticed for the first time what he was wearing—also pajama pants but striped blue and white ones and a white T-shirt. He was so sexy, so incredibly hot, in fact, that he might as well have been a model. I wondered for a brief second whether Malcolm used him as a model for his paintings.

"We match," I said, looking at his jammies and down at myself.

"In more ways than one, I hope," he said. "Get in. Join me."

I curled up next to him and rested my head on his chest where it was cozy and warm. I was even sweating from the bath and it didn't seem to matter to Sebastian. He held me in his muscular arms and made me feel protected, something I hadn't experienced in a long time. Maybe ever. Was it his age that made him so appealing that way? I couldn't figure it out. His money? I didn't want to admit it, but it was pretty special to be on this trip with him, all expenses paid, and at this incredible hotel in this massive king-sized bed that was actually fit for a king. But his money wouldn't have impressed me at all if I didn't like him. That I was sure of because Pete was broke and it hadn't stopped me from spending five years with him. It was something inherent in Sebastian—his desire to protect was strong. I noticed it from the first time I'd met him. It was subtle, the way he took care of my drink and matched it to my dress to make sure that I belonged, the way he kept his eye on me through the crowd. And now this. The way he came right over when he sensed I didn't want to be alone.

"How did you know?" I asked.

"Know what?" he said, like we didn't even need to have this conversation.

"Know that I wanted you here, that I craved having your arms around me."

"Sixth sense?" he joked. "I'm not sure. I could just tell."

He pulled me in and kissed the top of my head. Was this guy for real?

"Um," I started, "why are you perfect?"

"Am I perfect?"

"Yeah, this is perfect."

"Hmm. Well, let's see now. An incredibly intelligent, talented and sexy young woman seduces me on the phone with her unbridled passion and I have the most massive orgasm in history until I hear hers which puts mine to shame, so I ask if I can do what I can to join her for some afterglow. I don't know. Maybe it's you."

I moan softly. "Biggest orgasm in history?"

He nodded. "Yes."

"Bigger than you've had with anyone?"

"You have no idea what you do to me, do you?"

"I guess I don't."

"Well, let me tell you. Around you I'm alive."

"You do the same for me," I said. "When I saw myself tonight, how flushed I was after being with you, how wet I was, I took a good look at myself in the mirror and I felt sexy for the first time."

"Impossible."

"Why?"

"For the first time? You expect me to believe that?"

"I don't care if you believe it. It's the truth."

"Have you lived in a world with no mirrors, Claudia? You must have had hundreds of men throw themselves at you. You are a knockout. You don't know that, do you?"

"Not really."

"See? That I don't believe. Why even tonight, didn't you notice the way they all dropped their jaws in your direction?"

"They did?"

"They most certainly did. And I was the guy the other guys were jealous of. It was awesome."

"Did you just say 'awesome'?"

"I did." He laughed.

"You're hilarious."

"I can't help myself. This is one of those primal man things that you ladies don't know anything about. Forgive me for being a caveman for a moment but, yeah, it was awesome being the guy with the best-looking chick in the room."

I propped myself up and stared at him in disbelief. "You're serious, aren't you?" I finally asked.

"Dead serious. You are one hot mama and I have no idea what I did to deserve being in bed with you right now but I am very, very appreciative."

I couldn't help but laugh. "Mr Porter, are you objectifying me?"

"Are you offended?" His tone was suddenly solemn, like he didn't realize I was having fun with him.

"No. I'm amused. And surprised."

"Claudia Richards, I want to spoil you like you've never been spoiled before."

"Why?"

"Because it seems like you need it."

"What?" I was incredulous.

"You heard me. You need some pampering and that's all there is to it. I won't take no for an answer. It begins tomorrow. We're staying another day."

"Is that a fact?" I asked, unsure of how to interpret his tone. I was not used to having someone else call the shots.

"Oh, it's a fact. As your boss, it's also an order."

"You sure do know how to blur the boundaries, Sebastian. Mr Porter."

"Yes, it's strange business working for a private family. I can empathize. The Porters have a long history of giving out generous Christmas bonuses to those poor souls who put up with us. If you don't believe me, ask Anne Lise. She's been with us for over fifteen years."

"But have you slept with her?"

He looked at me sternly. "No. Heavens no."

"And here I am, employee and what? Lover? Something, anyway. These lines are awfully blurry to me."

"Then to hell with the lines. What do you want? Do you want to be my girlfriend? Then I'll spoil you with a Gold Card and expense account."

"And be your kept girl?"

"I can see the pride in your eyes, Claudia, and I respect it. If I had what you have, I might have made something of myself as a painter. Don't give it up because it's worth way more than any Gold Card will ever be. But that's also why I think you should let me spoil you."

"Wait. What?" I was trying to keep up not only with his compliments to me but with his unintentional jabs at himself. "Why do you say things like that about yourself?"

"Because they're true and I'm done hiding. I spent a good deal of my life pretending to be someone I wasn't and now I'm finally coming out of my shell and calling things as I see them. Just let me do it. It's part of my artistic process."

"Really?"

"Sure. Don't you think Van Gogh thought of himself as a failure, too? And don't you think he would have spoiled you if he could?"

"Well, yes to the first question but I'm iffy on the second."

"The thing is...it's okay for me to see my paintings as failures. It means I can move on. It's not some manifestation of low self-esteem, even though I know that's what it sounds like. It's been good for me to be here, to see Malcolm's exhibit with you. It's reinvigorated me."

"Really?"

"Yes. You're a powerful influence."

"I am?"

"Yeah. The way you looked at my paintings the other day. It was like you gave me permission to look at them again, too. And now I know what I need to do."

"What's that?"

"Change."

"What?"

"I'm not sure exactly how yet but I see things differently now and that's what I mean when I say you make me feel alive. You let me see things clearly. It's everything to me. So do I want to spoil you a little in exchange for that? Yes. Yes, I do."

"Well, when you put it like that."

"So tomorrow, I'm taking you shopping. Then you're going to the spa and when I think you've had all you can take, we're going to the best restaurant in Calgary, whatever that is. Probably a steakhouse, knowing this province."

"Wow." I couldn't say anything else. I was stupefied.

"And when we get back, I'm going back into my studio."

"Wow."

"You inspire me."

I was overwhelmed with joy and I held onto him so tightly the beating of his heart felt like my own.

"Will you stay with me tonight?"

"Do you want me to?" he asked.

I nodded.

"All right. Let's get some sleep."

We readjusted and he spooned me. If I'd wanted to, I could have squished my bum against him and felt his cock, but something about this evening was chaste and very romantic. I didn't want to ruin it. I was so curious about him. I couldn't wait to explore him physically, but I wanted to savor each and every moment. So I drifted off to sleep with his arms wrapped around me.

Never in my life had I felt so much at ease.

Chapter Five

In the morning, I woke up to find him dressed and sitting in a lounge chair reading the paper. I didn't move at first, just watched him as he alternated between reading and enjoying the view. He even looked in my direction a few times but I pretended to be asleep until I finally sat up.

"Good morning," he said. "I made coffee. Can I bring you a cup?"

"Mmm," I groaned, a little groggy still and trying to make sense of the night before. I couldn't believe he'd spent the night with me. I had slept with my boss. Literally. This was something to ponder, for sure. The strange thing was that I had dozed soundly. I hadn't expected to. Not that I had much experience staying over with guys I didn't know very well, but I remembered it had taken weeks before Pete and I had been able to actually drift off together. We'd often pushed and shoved each other accidentally, even long into the relationship. In retrospect, I should have considered it a red flag but that's the thing about hindsight.

"I was out like a light last night," I said when Sebastian came to my side and set down a tray with a cup, a small jug of cream and a bowl of sugar cubes.

"I'm glad. I don't know how you take your coffee so I had them bring everything. There's also some fruit and a couple of croissants, but I was thinking we'd go down and have breakfast in the restaurant. It's your call."

"It's all great, Sebastian. I take cream and sugar, but I can get that myself," I said, now sitting up and paying attention. I propped my pillows up so I could lean on them. "Did you have a good rest?"

"Yes."

"Oh good."

He stared at me intently before he added, "Actually, it was a terrible distraction having such a sexy vixen next to me. I did wake up a few times only to think I must be dreaming and when I realized you were here beside me, well, it was distracting."

"Oh no." I was saddened that he hadn't had the same experience I'd had but I didn't want to dwell on it because we were different. It was only natural we'd have different experiences.

"Don't worry," he said. "I'm usually a four to five hour sleeper anyway so I got a full night's rest."

"What time is it?"

"Ten."

"Oh." I blushed.

"You're more of an eight hour type, aren't you?"

I nodded, feeling self-conscious. Had he been killing time, wanting me to wake up? How embarrassing.

"When did you wake up?"

"Around seven."

"You should have gotten me up!"

"And disturb my precious sleeping beauty?"

"Well…"

"Never. It was a great thing to be able to enjoy the silence of the morning. I read the whole paper front to back. I don't often get to do that at home."

I wondered why not. For a brief instance a thought came to me that I couldn't deny. If I were rich, I told myself, I would only do what I wanted. Therefore, it was hard to believe that Sebastian couldn't just do whatever he felt like.

"Why not?"

"I usually go straight to work and then by afternoon the news isn't so new anymore. I mean, I get the headlines online throughout the day but it's nice to actually sit down and hold the morning paper and enjoy the view."

I held the mug in front of me. The familiar morning aroma was comforting.

"I talked to the concierge this morning and got recommendations for the best places to take you today."

"You're actually going through with that crazy plan of yours?"

"Of course."

"I thought that was just something you were saying last night. Sebastian, you don't need to spoil me. I'm not sure I'm even comfortable with the idea of it."

"Well, I am. I want to. Let me." He leaned toward me and brushed a stray lock of hair from my face. "I'll join you. I'll get a massage. I've got this kink in my back that I've been ignoring."

"Where? I'll rub it for you."

"You don't have to."

"I want to," I said and for fun I thought I'd imitate him. "Let me."

I put down my mug then caressed his back. He was so strong and lean. He was in excellent shape.

He moaned, instantly transporting me back to the sounds he'd made on the phone last night. I was becoming more and more aroused. I wanted to make a move on him but I held back. As I rubbed him, I had this nagging feeling that something about this was just too good to be true. How was this perfect man here in front of me and why was he insisting on spoiling me? *When did this become my life?* Only a few weeks ago I'd been waking up next to Pete and his stinky pile of boy laundry. We'd eaten macaroni and cheese and watched movies on the couch we'd found in the alley a few summers ago. It wasn't glamorous and it wasn't romantic. It was culture shock to be here.

Sebastian must have sensed my distance because he asked what I was thinking about and I pretended I was still sleepy. There was no way to describe to him how my life used to be and how weird it felt to be here with him. I was happy to be in his world and didn't want to think much about my old reality. *Forget those days,* I kept telling myself. *It's time to look forward.*

"I'm going to hop in the shower and get ready," I told him. "I have to look the part of the pampered princess if that's what I'm going to be today."

"That's the spirit," he said. "How about I see you downstairs for breakfast."

We agreed, and I went into the bathroom and immediately blushed when I looked at the tub with the showerhead resting in the bottom.

* * * *

Downstairs, I spotted him right away at a table in the corner. He was wearing jeans and a casual Polo shirt with horizontal blue stripes. This was not the Sebastian I was used to seeing and I liked it. It made me feel more at ease to see him relaxed and finally out of his suits.

I sat down across from him.

"Darn," he said.

"What?"

"I was hoping you'd sit down next to me so I could put my arm around you."

I blushed. "I know we sort of kind of had an intimate night last night," I whispered, "but I am nowhere near ready to sit on the same side of the table as you."

He gave me sad puppy dog eyes and said, "A man can dream, can't he?"

The server came and asked if I wanted coffee. I said yes. She smiled and I realized I was paranoid about being judged. I was sure the whole world — at least everyone in the restaurant — could tell we had spent the night together and had judgments about it.

"Have you decided on breakfast?" the server asked.

"Eggs benedict, please."

She turned her attention to Sebastian.

"I was going to be good and have the yogurt and fruit but now I'm rethinking." He paused, looking at me.

I felt like a bad influence.

"Nah, I better watch my waistline. Fruit and yogurt, please."

The server wrote down our orders then turned on her heel and rushed off.

"Oh no," I said. "Do you think I'm a pig?"

"There is nothing sexier than a woman with an appetite. I can't wait to watch you eat. But I am watching my diet. My doctor said no breakfast meats for me."

I liked that Sebastian took care of himself. It said a lot about a person if they cared what they ate. And, sure, I could have felt bad for ordering a rich meal but this was a day to remember. I had never had a day of pampering. I didn't even know what to expect but I was pretty sure that eating well was going to be part of it.

After breakfast, we took a leisurely stroll through the lobby and into the spa where two ladies in white greeted us.

"Sebastian Porter"—he extended his hand to the closest one—"and this is my, um. This is Claudia Richards."

Was he about to say girlfriend? Because it sure had sounded like he was. It felt amazing to think that one day, not too long from now, that was how he'd introduce us. I played it over again in my mind—'I'm Sebastian Porter and this is my girlfriend, Claudia Richards.' Oh yes, that sounded just perfect.

The woman shook our hands then took us to a room where there were two massage tables next to each other. The space was dimly lit with candles everywhere and there were two massage therapists ready for us. This was something I had never expected to experience. After selecting our choices of oil—we'd both chosen chocolate with peppermint for our temples—one of the massage therapists said, "All right, you two get undressed and get under your sheets and we'll knock in just a minute."

Undressed. Now that was something I had overlooked.

"For two people who had not yet seen each other naked, this was rather an intimate choice of activity," I said as soon as the door closed. "I'm shy."

"I won't peek. I promise."

"Turn around," I ordered.

And he did.

Soon I was slathered from head to toe in chocolate scented oil and every muscle was kneaded to the point where I became a giant slab of fudge, the kind I often stopped to watch at candy stores when candy makers slapped it around on a huge marble slab. With the peppermint on my temples, I felt even more like a minty chocolate truffle. For ninety minutes, we were on our backs, on our stomachs and in heaven. *What bliss.*

When it was all over, they asked if we wanted to shower together or apart and Sebastian looked at me as if to see whether my resistance had been kneaded right out of me. Then he said, "We better opt for separate."

Before his massage therapist took him to a different part of the spa, he whispered in my ear, "Think of me. I'll be thinking of you."

That comment went straight to my clit, in part because of the nearly public aspect of it. I mean, the two women were probably used to this sort of thing but it was far naughtier than I'd ever been.

Naturally, when I was in the shower, I gave myself a little stimulation in the form of my hand this time. There was something so inviting about touching myself with my skin slick from the oil. I had let go of everything bad that I'd been hanging onto. The new me was emerging full speed and again—it was foreign but welcome. How had I forgotten how good it felt to be touched? How had I survived an effectively sexless cohabitation with a man whose idea of romance was clean sheets? I tried to forget the many, many times Pete and I had a ten or fifteen minute tumble, and how he'd left me to take care of my own orgasm with my hand. I wondered if he'd have cared at all that I hadn't come. What had I been putting up with him for? It perplexed me. Now Penny was the one suffering through the minute-man and his television habits. Good riddance. I mean, no matter what happened with Sebastian, he had already treated me so much better than Pete ever had and if nothing else, this would be an exercise in raising my own standards.

Thinking that way—about the future, about the present, being right here with Sebastian right now—it made me aroused. I loved being in touch with my own sensuality, being the vixen who was comfortable enough in her own skin to give herself an orgasm at the spa. Up and down on my hard clit, I rubbed. The tension inside me rose, the need for release built and the wave of relaxation came over my throbbing clit. I longed to share my orgasm with Sebastian. I imagined being on top of him, riding his cock and touching myself, flicking my clit in front of him, watching him watch me with those gorgeously curious eyes. I wanted him to experience the way my pussy contracted. That was something Pete had told me about. It made me think of myself as special, like having a super power. Pete had once told me I was gripping him and I could feel it too when I came. I was enjoying the sensation of the muscles, eagerly fantasizing about gripping my Sebastian.

When I emerged from the shower, squeaky clean and completely relaxed, Sebastian was waiting for me in the lobby of the spa.

"Let me take you shopping," he said.

"Sebastian, it's too much."

"I am not going to let you refuse so just accept it. Whether you think of it as a work perk or something else is up to you."

I shrugged. There was no use in arguing, and actually I was delighting in this new reality of mine so why not see what he had in mind? We walked back through the Fairmont lobby and out into the daylight where the limo was waiting for us.

"Get in," Sebastian said.

I complied. This was weird. I mean, the last shopping spree I had gone on before I'd met Sebastian had been in thrift stores. I'd scored some good stuff, too, but still. Between that and Monique's closet, I barely wore anything that had not been broken in by somebody else first. But I couldn't tell Sebastian that. I guess I was afraid he'd be disappointed if he knew the truth.

When the limo pulled up to a little boutique, I got out and acted like it was perfectly natural. A woman in a stylish suit emerged from the two glass doors and welcomed us. This was a private shopping session, not at all like anything I'd tried before.

"Welcome to La Boucle," said the woman, extending her hand.

I shook it, unsure of how to act. I had completely fallen out of touch with the names of designers and I could tell from the ones etched into the windows that I was supposed to recognize them. No matter. I could just comment on cuts and colors and fabrics. I had learned that much from Monique and my brief stint reading fashion magazines in high school.

"I'm going to leave you here for a couple of hours," Sebastian said to me. Then he turned to the woman in the suit and said, "Please fix her up with a wardrobe she can enjoy and make sure she ends up with a dancing dress and pair of dancing shoes."

"Yes, sir. I will," the woman said.

Then he turned back to me and said, "For later."

I was terrified. I didn't know a foxtrot from a waltz. What kind of dancing was he thinking about? I was prepared to play along with being pampered, but he would discover two left feet if he looked down at mine. There was just no way around it. I gulped.

"See you in a while," he said.

"Um, okay."

Inside, the woman was much more relaxed. She introduced herself as Suzanne. She was a personal shopper and fashion consultant. She owned this luxury boutique and helped stars and rich people discover their own personal style. After she'd made a pot of herbal tea and passed me a mug, she told me to relax and let my personality shine.

"Being fashionable isn't about being trendy," she explained. "I aim to highlight my clients' personal features and unique expressions of their characters. Tell me about yourself."

"Let's see. I'm a Milton scholar working toward a PhD."

"Milton?"

"He wrote *Paradise Lost*."

"I've heard of it. It's a movie, right?"

"No."

"Well, never mind. I was never any good at English. So you work at a university?"

"Yeah."

She looked perplexed. "So how is it that you know Sebastian Porter?"

"Well, I just started working for him part time. I think it's temporary. I'm helping him with his philanthropy."

"I see."

All of a sudden I got the idea that she thought I was the object of Sebastian's philanthropy. I felt like Julia Roberts in *Pretty Woman*.

"So explain your personal style to me as you see it right now," she ordered.

"I...uh...I'm not sure I have one. Let's see. Well, right now I'm wearing this dress because, well, it's new." I couldn't tell her that this was also courtesy of Mr Sebastian Porter, could I? That without Sebastian, I'd likely be wearing my grungy old black turtleneck and my worn-in jeans that I'd had since I was nineteen. I'd have my hair in a ponytail and my nails manicured by my teeth.

"Would you say casual, then?"

"I guess." *That's putting it mildly. Slob was more like it.*

"What do your colleagues dress like?"

"Well, university professors tend to be pretty unstylish. Cords and cardigans. Stuff like that."

"My motto has always been that you should dress for the job you want, not the job you have. So where do you see yourself in five years? With the university or with Mr Porter?"

Aha! So she did think he was my sugar daddy. "Excuse me?"

I had no idea how else to answer her. It was torturous to have to confront such an empty blank space in my own inner being in front of this persistent person and I wasn't about to bare my soul to her. Couldn't she just put me in a few outfits, make me twirl around and be done with it?

"Look, it's been a while since clothes and stuff like that have mattered to me. No offense. For the past few years, my life has revolved around books and ideas and abstract stuff like that. I'm probably not at all like any of your other clients. I didn't even know places like this existed until we pulled up. Maybe I should just go."

That was it. Total shift in tone. She went from having her claws out to being downright maternal in her mannerisms as she put her hand on my arm. "No, no. I'm just trying to formulate an image."

"Well, that's just it. I'm not sure I want an image."

"You have one whether you want it or not."

"I stopped reading women's magazines a long time ago. I almost never go shopping."

"I hope I can change that for you. It should be fun to express yourself with what you wear. And you're a striking and beautiful young woman. You might as well show it off."

What was going on? Had the whole world suddenly decided I was pretty overnight? Where were all these people in my teens and twenties when I'd needed them? Maybe I'd become mousy because I didn't think I could be anything but that.

"Thank you. I guess I'm not used to hearing that."

"Hmm. That's surprising."

I was afraid to ask what she meant. She got up and walked across the store then came back with some pictures for me to look at.

"Which of these images appeal most to you?"

I flipped through some books with photos of women in various modeling poses, wearing everything from evening gowns to shorts and tank tops. I found one of a woman in jeans and turtleneck so I stopped. "This. Right here. This is my uniform."

"I see. So that would definitely fall under comfortable and casual. What kind of footwear do you pair it with?"

"I have boots, but sometimes I wear runners if I want to be cozy."

"Your boots. Do they have heels?"

"No. They're Doc Martens."

"I see." She sounded so disappointed.

"Like I said. I'm not that into my appearance."

For a minute she seemed deep in thought. Then she ordered me to stand up and undress. It was just the two of us in the store, she assured me.

Once I'd done what she said, she seemed even more perplexed.

"You have a great figure. You should be showing it off more. Let's try some things."

After that she started handing me stuff very rapidly. There were slacks and dresses, skirts and wrap-arounds, suits and jeggings. Everything. Monique would have been in Heaven, but I was starting to sweat and this was quickly turning into Hell.

"I've got it," she finally said. "You're a Katherine Hepburn."

"I am?" I did like her movies.

"Definitely. You've got that androgynous quality. You'd be very sexy in men's styles tailored for women. Vests and scarves and trousers will be perfect for you."

"That sounds very good."

"Cate Blanchett is also a Katherine Hepburn so if you're ever in doubt of what to wear, you can always pay attention to what she's wearing. See what kind of Katherine clothes are in season."

I knew I would be doing no such thing but I nodded politely. Within an hour, Suzanne had accumulated a giant pile of clothing matched to my personal style, which apparently was not too shabby after all. When Sebastian picked me up, he and Suzanne stealthily disappeared into a nook at the back of the room, and I watched out of the corner of my eye as he signed a document. Then we left. The clothes would all be tailored specifically to me and sent to the hotel later that evening, including my black dancing dress. I did get to tote the shoes out in a beautiful box.

"How much did you spend on me in there?" I inquired once we were in the limo.

"It doesn't matter. It was nothing."

"It matters to me."

"Well, not to me."

"Come on," I persisted. "I need to know how hard to work for you," I teased, hoping to convince him.

"If you must know, it was just over twenty, but you owe me nothing."

"Twenty?" I was perplexed. "As in thousand?"

He nodded. I thought my heart would pound itself right out of my chest. There were years that I'd lived on less than that. Whole years! I gulped and looked out of the window for a second, wondering if I should protest and call it off. Suzanne's tailors hadn't made a single incision yet. Maybe we could cancel the order and donate the money to the food bank. But I remembered my vow to let him treat me well.

"I must have good karma," I finally said. "Thank you."

"It's money well spent. After all, I get to see you in the new clothes, don't I?"

"Most definitely."

I felt like I should imply he'd get to see me out of them, too, but that would just trigger me. I was swiftly turning into Julia Roberts in *Pretty Woman*. Maybe I was supposed to take him for a barefoot walk in the park or something.

"When we get back, I want to make you dinner," I said, suddenly aware that that had always been my signature move. I'm a mean cook, especially of 'guy food', like steak and ribs.

"I'd like that," Sebastian said. "I'd like to see where you live."

"You mean where Monique lives. I still need to find a new place."

"I'd accept an invitation to Monique's in a heartbeat. And I insist that you let me help you with a place. I want you to live in a safe neighborhood."

"Well, I did," I said.

"Is that right?" He didn't sound convinced.

"Yeah. Despite what you may have heard, it's a great neighborhood."

"I'd prefer it if we found you a place near Monique."

"The rents there are much higher on that side of town."

"For good reason, Claudia."

The tone had been a little condescending and it was hard not to feel insulted and defensive. "Look, I've lived in my neighborhood for almost a decade. I've never had anything bad happen. I like it there and I feel more comfortable in a place that I'm able to afford on my own."

"But what about the newspaper headlines? It doesn't bother you that you live in a high crime area?"

"Only because of hypocritical laws and practices. There's more poverty, more people who get by on dealing marijuana dime bags and stuff like that. They aren't dangerous, just low income. Trust me."

"I don't want you living near drug addicts."

"Stop being so protective. I can handle myself," I scoffed. "Besides, there are drug addicts in every income bracket. The media just likes to make a big deal about the ones with other problems."

"I just care about you."

"I think you're a bit prejudiced."

"Against low income neighborhoods?"

I nodded.

"Have it your way," he relented. "But at least let me help you with transportation."

"You want to buy me my monthly subway pass now?"

"No," he laughed. "A car."

"I don't need a car."

"Sure you do. It's very inconvenient to get to my neighborhood on public transit and I don't like the idea of you walking home from your station late at night all by yourself."

"Well, like I said, nothing's ever happened."

"But if it did, I couldn't live with myself. I mean, buying you a car is really nothing to me."

"But it's a huge deal for me. And it's a little soon, don't you think?"

"You work for me. Why wouldn't I buy you a company car?"

"I'm fine. Really."

"Claudia, stop resisting. I just want to spoil you."

"But when you spoil me, it's like you erase who I really am. Don't you see? I don't actually live in your world, Sebastian." I couldn't hold myself back now. It was just like when we'd first met. "I'm doing my best to fit in with you but this is all way too much for me. I mean, twenty thousand dollars for clothes?"

"You don't enjoy them?"

"It's not that. They're beautiful and I am grateful. I really am. But I'd never be able to buy stuff like that for myself."

"Never say never," he said. "Besides, you don't have to. You have me."

"But—"

"Claudia, just take the spoiling."

"It makes me feel…" I couldn't finish the sentence. I couldn't say it out loud.

"How?"

"Like I owe you." *Wow. I said it.* The second the words had come out, it had felt wrong. I knew it wasn't how he saw me. I could tell. It was just so foreign for me to have a man buy things for me and treat me the way he did. It was something I hadn't even fantasized about because it had seemed totally unrealistic. Up until Monique's party, I had no idea that guys like Sebastian could ever cross paths with girls like me. I was enjoying it minute by minute, but I was unsure of where it was going. I was falling so hard for him. Maybe part of me needed to sabotage it, needed to push him away so that we couldn't go any further.

He stared at me, completely dumbfounded and silent. This was by a landslide the most awkward moment of my entire adult life. And it went on and on. My palms dampened. I wanted to open the car door and jump out, even in the middle of traffic.

"I see," Sebastian finally said. "Well, then I won't make you take anything." His voice was cold and distant.

I had clearly insulted him.

"Sebastian, I didn't mean for it to come out that way."

"How long have you been feeling this?"

"That's how I would feel if I let you set me up with a fancy apartment and a fancy car."

"Do you think I expect you to sleep with me for those things?"

"Not exactly."

"It says a lot about how you see me."

"I'm just not comfortable with you buying me stuff. That's not why I'm here with you."

"Why are you here?"

"Because I like you."

"But you think I'm trying to buy your love. That doesn't sound very honorable."

"I don't think that."

"That's what you implied just now."

"I didn't mean to." Was this guy hard to argue with or what? "I just don't want to get used to this luxury and then…"

"Then what? Are you already breaking up with me in your mind?" *Gah! He's impossible!*

"I just don't know you very well yet. We're moving pretty fast, don't you agree?"

"I don't know. Maybe."

"I think we are."

"Well, then we are. I'm an old man, Claudia. I get excited easily."

"Stop saying that. If I'm not allowed to say self-deprecating things, then you're not allowed to either." I crossed my arms.

"Fair enough."

"How old are you, anyway? I don't even know."

"Forty-two."

"That's not old."

"How old is your father?"

"It doesn't matter." Could this get any more awkward?

"How old, Claudia?"

"Fifty-two," I admitted.

"So I'm closer to him in age than I am to you."

"But it's totally different because he's old in his mindset but you're not." *And, well, because he is my father!* I knew it was time to stop the comparison because on no level did it feel like a good idea to continue.

"Are you close to your parents?" Sebastian probably wanted to change the subject, too.

"Um, I guess," I said, not wanting to elaborate, but then I considered what we had just been talking about and it seemed a great improvement to talk about family. "I always go home for Christmas and I usually try to see them once a month. They've been very supportive of me so, yeah, we're close."

"That sounds nice," he said. "My dad wasn't exactly a teddy bear dad but I understood him better after he passed away."

"I'm sorry," I interrupted. "When?"

"Oh, almost ten years ago now. He didn't care for 'the painting thing' and made certain I knew it. But after he passed away, I found a dossier amongst his things. He kept sketch books. He said nothing about it to me at all but all those years, he'd been drawing."

"Wow."

"Yeah. They were pretty good drawings, too. It all started to make sense after that, that his father before him had also been strict about going into finance and managing the family's estate. My grandfather was self-made. He came over here from England, penniless and determined, and he literally built an empire."

"What did he do?"

"He built houses. Then apartments. Then entire city blocks. Each time he sold, he invested in a new project and in other investments, too. He said one day he wanted to have his money work for him instead of having to work for money."

"That's impressive."

"Yeah, but he did it for my grandmother."

"Oh?"

"Yeah, she was from a wealthy family, very educated and pompous. Against her parents' wishes, my grandmother moved to Canada to be with my grandfather. This was only after he'd made his first small fortune."

"So the men in your family have been wooing women with money for generations?"

"Oh yes. My dad had this tradition of sending my mom flowers — huge bouquets of flowers — every single week. That was just habitual. Then there was jewelry, clothing, tickets to the opera, trips around the world. The Porter women have always enjoyed getting spoiled by the Porter men. It's tradition."

"Sebastian?"

"Yes?"

"Come here."

I grabbed him by the collar of his Polo shirt and pulled his face toward mine. Our lips met and I kissed him aggressively. It was so unlike me. Or maybe this was exactly like me. I was living the vixen fantasy. I was sure of one thing — the man beside me turned me on immensely. Did it matter what the future would bring? I finally believed I was truly sexy, truly desired. That was powerful. That was something worth pursuing.

Though I was swept up in the moment, my mind was still racing with thoughts of the future. I did my best to concentrate in spite of the weakness that came over me each time Sebastian kissed me.

"Your kisses are dangerous," I said. "I can hardly think."

"Do you need to think all the time?"

"I'm a scholar," I protested, but I appreciated his observation. Having identified myself as an over-thinker for some years now, I wanted nothing more than to trust my emotions. Yet we'd started a conversation that I wanted to finish.

"What are you pondering?" he asked.

"You got me questioning the future," I said. "Five-year plan. Ten-year plan. Kids. You know, life."

"And? Do you want kids?" he asked.

"I don't know." The admission shocked me. It had been easy to say with absolute resolution that I did not want kids before, but my situation had changed drastically. The end of my PhD was in sight and a marvelous man had come into my life. "Do you want more?"

"To be frank, I haven't considered it. I'm happy with Sarah."

"Did you and Deb stop for a reason, or did you want an only child?" Perhaps I was being invasive, but for some reason, this seemed important.

"Deb didn't have siblings and didn't miss them. When Sarah came into our lives, there was a sense of that being enough. It's hard to explain, but we never discussed having more."

"I see."

"When I was young, I didn't think I wanted to procreate at all. I thought it was selfish, maybe because I questioned my parents' motives to have me."

"That's kind of sinister."

"I was raised by nannies," he said by way of explanation. "So was Deb. We wanted to parent differently, take a more active role in Sarah's upbringing. Now she's at boarding school and sometimes I'm riddled with guilt that I'm repeating the family pattern."

"You were at boarding school, too?"

"Oh yes," he stated. "The best that money could buy. Semesters in Europe. Trips all around the world. No parental guidance."

The pain was palpable from his constant digs at his parents.

"You seem disappointed," I said.

"I'm not. When Sarah was born, I realized that all parents are failures in some fundamental way. We've been messing up the future generation since time immemorial. There's no sense in holding a grudge against the older generation just like there's no point in worrying about the precise way in which you're screwing up your own kid. You're bound to leave scars. It's natural. It's expected."

"You're not exactly selling me on the idea of having a family."

"Family is what you make of it. Biology is a factor, but not the only one. My personal definition of family is deeper than that. Take Hatia, for example."

"Monique," I said. Her name just came out, like a natural reflex to the word family.

"Exactly. Some friendships run deeper than the word allows." Sebastian had the air of a philosopher minus the pretense.

"So do you feel like your family is complete now?"

"If I ever feel that things are firmly complete, it'll be a sign that I'm closed off to the possibility of more. I don't know what the future holds, Claudia, and I won't pretend to know what it's like to be you. You're bright and caring and one day you might come to me and say you want to have a child."

"And what would you say if I did?"

"What I'm saying now. I have to remain open to possibilities. It's the only way to live," he took my hand and held it. "At this moment, I am happy to have one daughter. That could change."

"Just so you know, I've never pictured having children."

"You've been busy with your career, though."

"I'm just saying. I might not ever want them."

"We can't predict what lies ahead. All I know is that I cherish what is right here in front of me."

He lifted my hand to his lips and kissed the back of it.

Chapter Six

That evening at the hotel, he asked me to change into my dancing shoes and new dress. Clad in black, the femme fatale seductress I was becoming in my mind's eye turned into reality. We took the elevator to the mezzanine then curved down a corridor which led to a dance studio. A man named Murray met us and introduced himself as our tango instructor. I instantly started to sweat.

We were positioned in front of each other and Murray explained how the dance was meant to be one of seduction. *Perfect!*

"It's all about flirting and channeling your sexual energy and connection into your movements." He made eye contact with me when he spoke.

Could he tell that I was a ravenous temptress? Maybe he could.

Then he looked at Sebastian and said, "I want you to lead your woman backwards. Force her to step when you step."

The words were like butter to me, rich and inviting. Murray intervened and showed Sebastian what to do.

"Like this. Take her by the hand and connect with her elbow to elbow and then lead her," he instructed as he guided me forward and backward. "She wants to follow you. Don't forget that."

I couldn't argue there. And the way Murray talked about Sebastian leading me made me want to be led. There was no doubt about it.

When Sebastian and I were locked in an embrace again, Murray turned on the very sexy sounding tango music and helped us to learn the basics. I fumbled all over myself for the first few rounds but once I got the hang of it, I could tell that this was going to be a very seductive lesson indeed. I had no idea just how close two dancers' hips get to be when they tango. It was incredibly alluring.

By the end of the hour, Murray had us dancing. Perhaps we weren't gracious and perfect in our steps but we certainly weren't bad either. I was so surprised at myself that I actually had a left foot and right foot, and that they seemed to know what to do when the music came on.

"All right, my friends," Murray said as the hour drew to a close. "I have enjoyed this immensely and now I'll leave you to practice here for another thirty minutes. Please enjoy the space and the tango."

On his way out, he dimmed the lights.

"Do you remember what to do?" Sebastian asked.

I nodded. "I think so."

"Good," he said, sliding his right foot back so that I would have to follow him and step forward. Then he led me around the laminate floor, seducing me like the prince had to Cinderella when she'd gone to his ball.

There was such a magnetic pull between us. The tango expressed it perfectly. While we were swaying, it happened again — the dormant, dominant part of me woke up and I had to have him, right there on the dance floor. Even though we were all by ourselves it felt kind of taboo to reach up around his neck and pull him toward me. His lips were so soft and inviting. I could just stay there forever, feeling them against my own. I licked his upper lip gently to which he moaned.

"You drive me wild with desire," he whispered. "Just wild."

His words were an aphrodisiac. My pussy wet, my hips pressing into his, I wanted nothing more than to feel him completely, freed from the constraints of clothing. I wanted to be naked and horizontal with this man. I wanted that more than anything I'd ever wanted.

"Would you like to come up to my room?" I asked in my most seductive tone.

"What do you have in mind?" he asked. "Something naughty?"

"How could you tell?"

"Maybe I should go take a cold shower."

"Seriously?"

"Claudia, you know how I feel about you. I want this to work. I'm just thinking of us, of our future. I want us to be together. I'm trying to be good here, to be well behaved. I thought that's what you wanted."

"It is." I sighed. It may have been more like a huff.

"Well, isn't it?"

"It is but I want you really, really badly."

"Claudia, you naughty girl. You can't control yourself, can you? Here I thought I was the one who was being a bad influence but you're a dirty girl, aren't you?" he whispered in my ear.

My clit pounded. I longed to feel his hands all over my body. I nodded. *Yes, Sebastian, I am a dirty, dirty girl.*

"You're turned on right now, aren't you?" It was like he could see right through me.

I nodded again. Then I took his hand and lifted my dress up to reveal to him that all this time I hadn't been wearing any underwear.

"Claudia," he gasped. "I had no idea you were so...so...slutty."

That was it. The sound of his voice when he said the word *slutty* so slowly and seductively was too much for me to handle. I couldn't stand the state of my untouched pussy any longer. I needed him to know how desperate I was. I took his hand and guided it to my wetness. He touched me. His skin harder than my own, his hands sexy and manly. He moaned deeply as he fondled me. He couldn't help himself either. His finger entered my pussy and it was so good, so welcome. I was aching by then and needed to be touched. I moaned and kissed him again. He penetrated me deeper and deeper.

"You're a slutty girl, aren't you?" he asked, again with that tone that drove me crazy.

"Yes."

"Tell me what you're thinking about."

"About you fucking me with your cock."

He moaned. "Uh-huh."

"Mm hmm. I've been thinking about nothing but fucking you ever since we got here."

"Claudia," he said. "You are so sexy right now. Do you know that?"

I looked down, feeling shy at his words. Then I saw what he was doing to me. The vision was even more arousing than the feeling. Or at least the sight of his finger entering me made the sensations even more intense. I could no longer see his hand beneath me as his finger glided inside. My pussy was so welcoming I felt like I could grab onto him and pull him into me and never let him go. He fucked me like that for minutes, both of us stupefied and staring, watching what was happening as though it was in slow motion.

He paused, pulled his finger out then slowly lifted it to his face. Seductively, he took it into his mouth. "Mmm," he said. "You taste good."

"Come upstairs," I said.

"Claudia."

"I need you to lick my pussy."

He said, "Do you want to make me come in my pants like a schoolboy? When did you turn into such a slut?"

"I can't help myself around you."

"I see."

"I want you to taste me."

He nodded. "I want nothing more than to taste your sweet juices and lick you all over."

"I've been fantasizing about your tongue." I didn't know where this was all coming from or how I was able to say it. I'd never been able to express my sexual desires before yet now the words were pouring out of me as effortlessly as the wetness from my pussy.

"You have?"

"Yeah, your strong tongue that I'd love to feel in my mouth…"

"Yes?"

"I want you to make me come with your tongue."

"You do?"

I nodded. "You're right about me. I'm a slutty, slutty girl."

"My, my."

"Will you let me come?" I pleaded, again batting my lashes.

"How can I say no to you?"

He led me out of the dance studio and to the elevator. When the doors parted, we got in. We were alone, thankfully, and he pushed me up against the wall where he leaned into me as he kissed me deeply and passionately.

"Claudia, you're so sexy, so incredibly sexy. I don't believe how lucky I am."

His cock hardened. It teased my pussy. My pussy wanted his cock. It was independent of my brain completely. It was animal instinct.

We fumbled out of the elevator into my room and went straight to my bed where he pushed me down on my back and spread my legs open wide. Before I even knew what was happening, he had his tongue inside me, forcing his way deep into my cunt. I moaned in ecstasy. I didn't think he'd relent and I was so grateful, so incredibly turned on and so blissed out I could barely see straight. I closed my eyes and just let him explore me while I moaned. Minutes went by like this until I reached for his zipper, straining myself. I was ready to take his cock in my mouth, suck on him and make him feel how badly I wanted him.

He stopped what he was doing. "No, no. You wanted me to make you come like this and that's what you're going to get. That and nothing else."

Now this was a first. A man that did not think with his cock even when it was as hard as Sebastian's was in that minute. He was part of a species that I hadn't known existed. All I could do was moan my reply. He went back to licking my pussy. It was as though he had taken lessons in my specific anatomy, as though he could read my mind completely. How did he know exactly how I liked it? He used the surface of his tongue instead of the tip and moved it up and down, applying just the slightest pressure.

I was in ecstasy and released a dramatic gasp as his finger slid deep inside, like I'd forgotten to breathe. He thrust in and out in perfect harmony with the rhythm of his tongue. He took his time, too. There was no sense of rush. It was exactly as he had said. He was going to make me come this way and all I had to do was surrender to it. There was nothing else. He was going to lead and I was going to follow and that was that. So I did exactly as he wanted because it happened to be precisely what I wanted. I released my breasts from the shackles of my push-up bra, which was easy enough since I was on my back. I took each nipple between my forefinger and thumb the way I liked to do when I masturbated. The thing was, though, that I'd never gotten up the nerve to do this in front of a man and I never thought I would. Ever.

He stared up at me and gave me a look that told me just how much he enjoyed it. That encouraged me and I squeezed myself harder as he thrust in and out of my wet pussy. The sound of his touch seduced me into closing my eyes and paying attention only to the way things felt, and when I did, I completely let go. Never had I been so stimulated — both nipples with my own fingers, my clit with his tongue, and my pussy with his finger. After I'd lost all sense of time, I gave in to a massive, pulsating orgasm. My pussy tightened around his finger and let go of all of that sexual tension. Tightened and released. Tightened and released. Over and over. He kept his finger inside me and watched in disbelief. I felt so exquisite, so divine and complete. After my orgasm, I collapsed entirely. It was like I was falling, falling. And he lay down beside me and held me close. He licked my pussy juices slowly off his fingers then with his wrist he wiped the sweat from my brow.

"You're beautiful," he said.

And I fell asleep in his arms, feeling bliss like I'd never known.

Chapter Seven

Back in Toronto, I waited patiently for Monique to get home. When the door finally opened and she walked in, her first statement was, "Tell me everything."

"Oh my God, Monique. I don't even know where to begin."

"Hold on," she interrupted. "Is that a Stella McCartney blouse?"

I nodded.

"You whore," she joked. "I guess you don't have to tell me everything. I can see for myself."

"Oh, stop. It's not like that."

She lifted an eyebrow at me. She had perfected the expression that said — *you're busted*.

"Really," I insisted. "We, uh — I think I'm in love."

She sat down and wrapped her arms around me in a congratulatory way. But then her expression changed. She pulled back.

"What about his wife?" She looked serious.

"They're getting divorced, actually."

She went from sad-news-story-face to day-at-the-circus-face in no time. "Sweet. When does she move out and when do you move in?"

"Monique!"

"What? It's a valid question."

"I don't think she'll be moving out at all."

"What?"

"This has to stay in the vault," I said. This was our code for total secrecy.

"Of course," she said.

"I mean it. Like not a peep. I'd be devastated if Sebastian found out I told you," I said. I couldn't even believe I was saying anything, but Monique was the closest person I had to a sister.

"Vaulted. One hundred percent." She put her hand on her heart in confirmation. "Now continue. I'm dying here."

"They're sort of unconventional. They still love each other but more like friends now than before."

"Weird."

"It turns out that his wife actually has another lover. Partner, really. A woman she's been with for years."

"She's a lesbian?" Monique's phone buzzed in her briefcase. Normally, she'd check the message right away, but she left it alone. This was good gossip, and she didn't want to miss it.

"Bisexual."

"And Sebastian was okay with her cheating?"

"She wasn't cheating. They had an open marriage." I tried to avoid sensationalizing the news, but Monique's attentiveness made it clear she wanted the *People* magazine version.

"Ha!" she bellowed. "That's what they all say. I'm opening a bottle of merlot and that's the only kind of open I understand."

She got up and went into the kitchen, got two stemless wine glasses out of her sleek glass cupboard, took the corkscrew from the drawer and reached for a red wine from the rack on the wall.

"Really," I said. "He wants me to meet her. Them."

She poured the wine into the glasses and without even clinking with me, lifted hers then took a sip.

"Are you going to?" She sat back down and crossed her legs on the sofa and leaned forward, like she was ready for me to confide anything.

"Sure. Why not? I mean, I like him a lot."

"Sounds complicated."

I sipped. "That's my biggest hesitation." I told her everything there was to tell—about Sarah, about the threesome, and Nadia.

"Sounds like he's being honest and wants you to know everything."

"Yeah." I nodded. "Somehow the complications don't seem like a big deal anymore. I'm actually kind of looking forward to meeting the family, even just to see what they're like."

"You know, I have to say that I respect a man who is able to support his wife while she explores her sexuality. That takes balls."

"I know, right?" My heart swooned at the thought of Sebastian.

"I suppose he bought you that." She gestured at the blouse and then at my Katherine Hepburn slacks.

"He did," I sighed. "He said he loves buying me stuff."

"Shut up!" Monique's tone totally changed as she almost spat her wine all over my outfit that cost about the price of tuition for a semester at U of T.

"I know. Weird, right?"

"Lucky is more like it."

It took about an hour before I stopped divulging the intimate details. I made her swear one more time that she'd never tell. Finally, after we'd each had a glass and a half of merlot, she looked at me and said, "Claudia, you're in love."

My bashful smile betrayed me.

"That is so great," she said. "It sounds like he genuinely cares for you. And, hell, the benefits are amazing." She petted my arm — only she was feeling the fabric.

"Do you want to see the other benefits?"

Her eyes lit up. It was nice to just give in to the excitement of having all these new things. It was true what we'd talked about in the car back in Calgary. I didn't have to overthink it. I could just enjoy it. After all, how many times in life would I go on a shopping spree like that? And there really was nothing better than sharing such luxurious memories with my best friend.

I opened my suitcase, and she took over from there, pulling out item after luxurious item, gasping with delight at each one. I told her about Suzanne and Katherine Hepburn and felt like my life was finally normal again, now that I was back here with her.

"So what's new with you?" I asked after realizing I'd monopolized the conversation for way too long.

She shrugged emphatically. "Meh."

"What happened?"

"Nothing. That's the problem. I wore this to work." She gestured at her miniskirt with dangling chains in the front. She'd paired it with a cute leather jacket that looked like something a K-Pop star would wear. "And still all I got from Jerome was a 'Good morning, Monique. Did you get my email about the Swanson file?'" She rolled her eyes like she was telling me about the world's most irritating coworker. "It's like he completely doesn't remember what happened."

Jerome had apparently kept Monique late one night when she'd worked under him and they'd shared a moment and supposedly almost kissed. But Monique discredited the story saying it might have been mostly in her own head. She did have a tendency toward drama and she'd been in love with Jerome for a long time.

"Men can be such twerps," I said, filling her glass with the remainder of the merlot. "You look hot and he's an idiot if he didn't notice."

* * * *

The next day, I got showered and dressed in my slacks and blouse with a cute blazer—the most unassuming of all the outfits Sebastian had bought for me. I put my hair back in a simple ponytail and didn't do anything out of the ordinary with my makeup. I had to go the university to do some paperwork that I couldn't do from home. Plus, there was an optional department meeting, and I figured it was in my best interest to go to everything I could.

When I got there, Janet, one of the Chaucer professors who rarely talked to me, came right up to me and said, "Claudia, did you lose weight or something? You look amazing."

I said I hadn't, but it felt great to be noticed that way. Then it happened again. Paul, one of the literary criticism profs, was mid-conversation with another faculty member when they both suddenly stopped then turned and stared at me.

"What happened to you?" Paul asked.

He and I have had a number of good connections at the department pub nights at the faculty lounge but this was still pretty blatant considering we were colleagues, not friends.

"Um, what?" I was suddenly shy about my new attire.

"You clean up nicely, Richards," he said, punctuating his comment with his charming grin.

Was he flirting with me?

"Uh, thanks."

"Did you hear there's a new position opening up in the department?"

"No." But I sure loved being including in department gossip.

"Yeah, Frank said they got funding for another faculty member but they haven't chosen yet. They're probably going to keep it pretty quiet, but you should apply," Paul said.

"Well, how do I apply if they are keeping it quiet? Won't it be obvious I heard it through some gossip then?"

"Just figure it out, Richards," he said. "Everyone wants to keep you around."

He hadn't been so sweet to me before. Suzanne was right. Dressing the part was actually kind of a good idea. I was starting to understand how mousy people got overlooked because the old me would have quietly slipped into my little office and not made small talk.

* * * *

That night, Sebastian's driver, Adam, picked me up and took me to another part of town I barely visited. I was starting to see that I didn't know Toronto at all. I knew the part of the city that I could afford, and that was limited to the main districts. We drove to the outskirts and down a secluded road that seemed like a private driveway to an aristocrat's abbey, but at the end of the road there was a gorgeous restaurant. I was glad I'd worn my wrap-around dress. Thrift store chic would not have cut it.

At dinner, I told Sebastian all about the news at school as I studied the exposed brick walls in our cozy little booth. The place was called Malbec because they specialized in the Argentine wine. He ordered a bottle and I tried not to think about how it cost about as much as my monthly food budget used to be before I'd started going around with Sebastian. It was strange how quickly my circumstances had changed.

"To your brilliant career," he said after he held up his glass and examined it closely.

"I haven't got the job yet, but thanks. And cheers." I clinked glasses with him. The wine was pungent with a distinctive oak flavor. I swirled it around in my mouth and savored it. This was a real treat, easily worth a month of groceries.

"You will," he said. "I have a good feeling about it."

"Why?"

"Because things are looking up for you on all fronts." He smiled.

I was instantly charmed. Indeed, things were on the upswing. He ordered Argentine style tapas for us. I didn't even look at the menu and I didn't have to. I was Sebastian Porter's date. Before the food arrived, the chef came out from the back and hugged him.

"Juan, this is Claudia," he introduced me.

I put my hand out to shake his. Juan took it and kissed it.

"Claudia, I hope you love your meal. I'm preparing it just for you."

"I'm sure it'll be delicious," I said.

"It always is," Sebastian added and sat back down. Juan left us after that and Sebastian said, "He's a real artist. Painting is one thing. Wait until you see his dishes."

"Oooh," I cooed. "I'm looking forward to it."

Under the table, Sebastian put his hand on my lap, cupped the top of my thigh, and squeezed. I almost jumped up. I've never been one for public affection and even though this was well-hidden, I was on guard.

"You're so sexy when you're shy," he whispered.

"Sebastian," I protested in a hushed voice. "I'm shy because I'm uncomfortable. There are people everywhere," I spoke through clenched teeth, exaggerating my discomfort. I liked that he wanted to touch me. And in his defense, our booth was quite secluded.

"Oh, I see. So it would be wrong of me to do this?" He found the hem of my dress and put his hand on my thigh underneath it.

Still through clenched teeth I said, "Sebastian, you're a bad boy."

"I can't help it."

"Stop it," I said, but I didn't mean it. What I meant was—*you're turning me on.*

He was cautious suddenly. "Okay."

I shook my head. "I love that you can't keep your hands off me," I confessed.

"Oh, really?" He was such a flirt.

I nodded. "Yes, really." Changing the subject, I asked, "When is Deb coming home?"

"Soon. In a week."

"A whole week?"

"What's the matter? You don't think you can wait that long?"

I shook my head. "I know I can't."

The server brought our first course—burrata and prosciutto on toasted rusks drizzled with olive oil. It looked fattening and amazing. We took our flirting down a notch to savor the first bite. It was like a little cloud from Heaven had landed on my tongue.

"This cheese," I mumbled. "It's so soft."

"Like your lips," he said and then he took a sexy bite.

Why was it that everything he did was sexy? I couldn't figure it out. He just turned me on so much that it didn't matter if he were actually doing something sexual or if he was just eating. It must be lust, I figured.

After dinner, we got into his car and took a drive. For once, Sebastian was in the driver's seat. Adam was still on duty and would be taking us home, but Sebastian requested that we take the car over the lookout point alone. It wasn't far from the restaurant. We could practically have walked, though something told me Sebastian preferred not to do anything pedestrian.

"I wasn't sure you could drive," I teased.

"Claudia, just because a man prefers to be driven does not mean he doesn't know how to drive. Anyway, tonight I wanted to have a traditional date with you."

"Nothing I've experienced with you has been traditional."

"Oh?"

"Well, yeah."

"What kind of things have you traditionally done on dates?"

"Well, never mind about that."

"I'm curious."

"Don't be."

But he insisted, "Tell me."

"Fine. Pete and I were both broke so we didn't do anything exciting. We never went to places like Malbec, if you must know. Instead, we improvised and made our own entertainment with simple things. Like there was this time I made him a picnic dinner and we sat and watched the sunset. It was nice."

"With you anything would be divine."

I smiled. "Once, he told me to meet him in the park and he showed up with a tub of Häagen Dazs and two spoons. That was very cute."

"Hmmm." Sebastian seemed kind of distant for a second.

"What is it?"

"I wonder if you'd do things like that with me."

"What do you mean?"

"I mean, I'm different, aren't I? All my life I've felt like I couldn't actually do the stuff that regular people do." He sounded so dramatic, like he was royalty or something.

"Excuse me? Regular people?" My posture stiffened. "It's not like you grew up in a bubble or anything."

"I sort of did. I was sent to all the best academies, pushed to achieve, to excel at business so I could take over the family empire. I had to date within my parents' circles. Deborah is my mom's best friend's daughter. We knew from a very early age that if we didn't hate each other, we'd probably end up together."

"Like royalty."

"Don't make fun, Claudia. I'm being serious. I'm trying to share something vulnerable with you that I generally don't talk about because it sounds so goddamn pretentious."

"Sorry."

"All my life I've wanted things to be simple."

"Couldn't you just opt for simplicity in your own way?"

"Not with all those expectations."

"So you and Deb never had movie nights where you made Rice Krispies squares and sat around in sweat pants?"

"No." He turned to me and examined me like I was talking about the most exotic experience in the world.

"Never? Not in thirteen years of marriage?" I was incredulous.

"I don't think she has ever cooked a meal for me. I've never cooked, either, nor have I done anything like bring ice cream to the park. It's not right, Claudia. I see that now. I want those things."

"Well, if you want me to cook for you, just ask."

"I suppose that's what I'm doing."

"Okay, mister," I said, "next Saturday night at Monique's. She's going to be out until late. But you can't stay over, because the couch is not big enough for two."

"Of course," he said. "When do you think you'll have your own place?"

"Sebastian, not this again," I huffed. "I looked at a few apartments in the neighborhood you like and they're all so…"

"So…what?"

Ridiculously overpriced! "It's hard for me to picture myself there."

"Why? You're about to be a professor of literature at one of Canada's finest universities. When are you going to start taking yourself seriously?"

"I don't think my address has anything to do with whether I take myself seriously."

"Look at Monique. She's doing well for herself, and she also lives a certain lifestyle. And you can afford it now."

"Sebastian, please stop with the mixed messages. You say you want simplicity and yet you tell me I'm not palatable to you unless I live in the right neighborhood."

"That's not what I said."

"It's what you think." I crossed my arms and took in more of the view.

This was a stunning city on a beautiful evening, and suddenly I felt guilty that I got to see it from this angle. I thought about the girl I used to pass every day on my way to school. She was always right outside the subway station with her cat on a leash and her tin can out. I'd got in the habit of tossing her a few coins every day, but it seemed like a futile cycle. Now and then, when I remembered to, I'd bring a can of cat food and we'd make eye contact for a little longer than usual. Even though I never knew her name, she meant a lot to me. She was part of my community, and I didn't know if I'd ever get Sebastian to understand what that was like.

"What I think is that I want you to be safe and, yes, I want you to see yourself the way I see you, as an up-and-coming professional."

I walked back to the car. Sebastian followed and opened the door for me. "I'm a scholar. Scholars don't care about image. It's a thing. Trust me."

"Trust me when I tell you you're wrong. Everything is about who you know and what people think of you."

"Maybe if you're one of those prestigious academy types, but not where I'm from. Let's just drop it."

"I asked Anne Lise to look into it and rent a place for you."

"You didn't." I didn't know what else to say.

"Don't be mad, Claudia," he pleaded. "She found a place and put a deposit on it. That's where we're headed right now."

"What?"

He pulled up in front of the restaurant and we both got into the back seat. Adam returned to duty. Part of me was fuming and another part of me was thrilled to know he thought of me when we weren't together.

"Reserve your scowl until after you see the place. Please?"

"Sebastian, you have no right to interfere in my life like that. I'll make my own choices about where to live." My voice was low but firm.

"You don't have to take it. I just want you to see it."

"But you already put a deposit on it."

"It doesn't matter. It's nothing to me."

I thought of the nameless girl again and wondered what a difference a sum like that would make in her world.

"Well, not to me," I said. "Look, I don't think you realize just how different we are. I've been trying to downplay it because I want to get used to being pampered. I love the way you treat me, but I feel weird about the money factor. When I first met you, I was so smitten and then I thought I'd let you be nice to me because I need that. I told myself I'd earned it. I've put in plenty of years of being an overlooked mousy Frumpzilla so, sure, I'll let this guy spoil me. What's the harm?"

Where was this all coming from and why couldn't I make it stop?

"But it's too much. The clothes you bought me. They're so nice but you know what? My last shopping spree was at the Sally Ann. The Sally Ann!"

"Then I don't understand why you don't let me treat you. Unless of course you like shopping at the Sally Ann."

"That's not the point. I mean, I do like it sometimes, but that's neither here nor there. We're from different worlds. I can't just put down money and decide to take this glitzy apartment because what am I going to do in three months when you're tired of me and decide to break up with me?"

"Claudia!" Sebastian asked Adam to pull the car over to the side of the road.

I was crying. This was easily the most vulnerable I'd made myself so far. "I'm sorry. Look, I appreciate what you're trying to do but it's too much. It's too soon. What if Deb and Sarah don't like me?"

"They'll love you and I have no intention of breaking up with you, and anyway, you can afford it because you're on salary at Porter & Sons and you're about to be a tenure track professor."

"I can't be so sure. There are lots of people they could give the position to."

"You'll get it," he said. "I have faith in you. You're smart and you've worked hard."

He held me in his arms. It felt so good that he believed in me and I wished I could believe in myself like that.

"Sebastian?" I looked up at him, wiping my teary eyes. "I get what you're doing. I get that you're just trying to be nice. I'm just not used to it but I'm going to try."

"Yes, try. Now let me take you to the place that could be your new home, if you want it."

"Okay."

He held me in his arms for a while and tucked a few strands of hair behind my ear. He caressed my cheek. It was impossible to stay mad at him.

We pulled into the gated garage area, and I had no idea what to expect. The elevator was all chrome and showed that the glass tower had thirty-two floors. Sebastian pressed the lobby button.

We got out of the elevator and I almost passed out. The place was like the Fairmont lobby—there was a small table in the center of the room with a massive bouquet of huge flowers. The concierge nodded in our direction and Sebastian introduced himself to the security guard who pushed a button behind the counter.

Within minutes a well-dressed woman in her fifties extended her hand to me. "I'm Barbara," she said, "the building manager. Here is your key." She handed it to me. "Please let me know if you have any questions."

"Thank you," I said, unsure of myself. *Will any of my alley furniture fit in here? I highly doubt it.* But I reminded myself that Sebastian had arranged this to show me how much he cared. I owed it to him to keep an open mind.

"Sebastian, this place is like a hotel," I said on the way back to the elevator.

"It is. And you like hotels as far as I can tell."

He pushed the button to the twenty-seventh floor. I gulped. I had major butterflies in my stomach and hoped somehow that the place would be a tiny hovel in the sky. This was all too opulent for me.

I turned the key and unlocked the door and walked in and found the lights right away. "Holy shit!" I yelled in spite of myself.

"Do you like it?"

I ran—literally ran—into the living room that was furnished with two huge leather sofas and a seventies style large chrome lamp that was suspended from an arched chrome beam that was connected to the wall. Everything was modern and minimalist in shades of gray and white.

The view was incredible. The city sparkled below. The kitchen was big and had all glass cabinets and gray marble counters. The dining table looked like it should be in a fancy restaurant. The four chairs were made of steel with tall backs. There was a gorgeous bouquet in the middle of the table.

"Do you like it?" Sebastian asked.

"Like it? I love it. I'm speechless," I said.

"Wait until you see the bedroom."

"There's more?"

"Oh yes. There's a bedroom, an office and the bathroom. I think you will especially appreciate the bathroom."

He took my hand and led me to through my very own palace, and as strange as it felt to be here, it certainly also felt like something I could get used to. The bedroom was huge and had its own en-suite washroom. At first I assumed that was the bathroom he'd been talking about but it turned out that there was a massive bathroom down the hallway that had a Jacuzzi tub and that very familiar large detachable showerhead in stainless steel. The sink was the kind that looked like a glass basin sitting on a counter. Beneath it, there was a rock surface, like the beach had inspired the designer. I recalled the spa in Calgary. I couldn't believe that this could be my new reality. *But why resist it?*

The office was furnished with bookshelves and a desk overlooking the city. The whole apartment featured floor-to-ceiling windows and I was just astounded to be here.

"Do you think you could get used to this?"

"Sebastian, you are a bad boy, spoiling me like this."

"So do you?"

I nodded. In spite of my misgivings, the only word I could utter was, "Yes."

"Then it's settled. You can move in effective immediately and make me dinner here on Saturday night. And, maybe if I'm good, you'll let me stay over."

"You can definitely stay over." I winked.

I couldn't believe things could be this easy. It was just too good. I shook my head.

"What is it?" Sebastian asked. He sure was perceptive.

"It's just that I feel so cared for."

"Good" — he smiled — "that's how I want you to feel."

"Oh my God. What will I tell my parents?" I started to freak out a little in my head. "That my rich boyfriend got me this fancy apartment?" It occurred to me that I dropped the b-bomb and I covered my mouth.

Sebastian laughed. "You can tell them you're successful. That's all you have to say, isn't it?"

He totally ignored the boyfriend comment and I wondered if it was because he was uncomfortable. He took my hand and led me to my living room. We sat down on the couch.

"Would you want to meet them?" I asked. "My parents?"

"Sure," he said. "When do you think is a good time?"

"I, uh, I don't know. I mean, I can't hide this lifestyle change from them forever but last time I talked to them I told them Pete and I were over and I don't think it's cool in their eyes if our very next conversation revolves around my meeting this handsome and generous, older still-somewhat-married guy."

"I see."

"I mean, I just don't know how it'll sound to them."

"So you're reluctant?" He seemed worried.

I wanted to comfort him, but the truth was that I didn't know how to broach it with them.

"I don't fully know what to say yet, if that's what you're asking."

"Did they like Pete?" He leaned back, like he was defensive.

I wished I'd called my parents more in the past few weeks, but everything had moved so quickly. There was no way for me to reassure him.

"They did. He and my dad bonded over politics. My mom liked that he was a good cook," I said, hoping I wasn't hurting Sebastian's feelings especially since he'd just revealed he wasn't exactly much of a chef himself.

"I see." He got up and walked to the living room.

I followed.

"I'm sure they'll love you," I said.

"The older married guy who enjoys spending money on their daughter." He smirked. "Yeah, I'm sure they'll love me." He sat back down on the couch with a sigh.

His sarcasm saddened me.

"I didn't mean to put it like that and they won't see it like that. I just have to present it to them a little differently."

"How?"

"I'm not sure yet."

"Do you think you'd like to refer to me as your boyfriend?"

"Um—" I panicked just a little. He *had* noticed. I blushed. "Yeah, I would like that because I sort of think of you that way already."

He leaped up and put his arms around me and held me tight. "Claudia, it's an honor to be your boyfriend."

"Well, can you be that?"

"Sure. Why not?"

I touched his wedding ring again.

"Just labels. All of it. I mean, we can call each other whatever we damn well please, I think. Don't you?"

"Yes. I just want you to know, too, that my parents are really cool people. They aren't conventional. They aren't judgmental. All they care about is that they guy I'm with is good to me." I hadn't exactly been forthcoming about Pete. I still needed to tell my parents why we'd broken up. I'd fallen so far behind on phone calls, caught up as I was in the whirlwind of new romance.

"Am I good to you?" he asked. He was being sincere.

"Yes, Sebastian."

We kissed. His lips felt so right, so perfect against my own. I loved the feeling of being in his embrace.

This was my new life and this incredible man was here in my new sexy apartment that I couldn't wait to show Monique. Everything had changed in the last month. Absolutely everything. On the surface, I had new luxuries in my life, the clothes, this sofa, this apartment, Sebastian, but it was more profound, too. I didn't want to settle anymore. I looked back on my old self with disdain and wondered how I had ever lived that way. There was no point in dwelling on the past when it would be a million times more fun to inaugurate my apartment. I straddled Sebastian. He was taken aback.

"What are you doing?"

"I'm finishing what I started back on that leather sofa in Calgary."

"Here?"

"Yes. It's my place, isn't it? So I can do what I want."

"I've created a monster, haven't I?"

"We'll see," I said coyly.

Then I leaned in and kissed him. My skirt was almost up around my waist in order to wrap my legs around him, and he held me in his strong arms and rubbed the sides of my legs with his palms. He was so good at holding me. Our bodies fit together perfectly. I couldn't help but see it as a sign. I felt sexy around Sebastian. He brought it out in me in ways that no one else had.

"Claudia, you're so sexy," he said when I pulled back from the kiss and looked into his eyes. "I mean it. I can't believe you're in my life. I've been turned on twenty-four-seven ever since that day at the corporate function when I saw you in that dress."

"Yeah, it was pretty sexy, wasn't it?"

"He nodded."

"You know what?"

"What?"

"Right before I got to the party, I went to Monique's and had a shower there and shaved my pussy.

Monique has one of those detachable showerheads like at the Fairmont."

As I was talking, Sebastian had to readjust to accommodate his growing member, an enthusiastic response to my storytelling.

"You mean you had a silky smooth pussy under that sexy satin dress of yours?"

I nodded. "And I was so wet all night because I'd made myself come in the shower and I was so turned on."

"Oh my God. Claudia, what you do to a man. I didn't stand a chance."

"Me?" I feigned innocence.

"Yes, you, you dirty girl," he said, his voice stern. "I ought to punish you for making me walk around with a constant erection. It's not nice of you, you know. But that's why you do it, isn't it?"

"Maybe."

I sat back just a little and undid the top button of my blouse. I also took my hair out of the simple ponytail and gave my head a good toss, like a librarian about to get naughty. His eyes got bigger as he tried to sneak a peek into my shirt.

"Oh, you like what you see?"

He nodded. "Oh, yes. Very much."

"How about this?" I unbuttoned a couple more and revealed my cleavage.

He pulled me in and kissed my skin.

"You smell divine," he whispered. "I could kiss you everywhere."

"Everywhere?"

"Claudia, you're torturing me. I thought we agreed to take it slow. I can't resist you. You're too much."

"Oh yeah?" I said, unbuttoning the final three buttons of my blouse. I took it off so I was just wearing my lacy pink bra.

"Yes." He nodded. "Look at you. You're like a porn star. No, wait. You're way hotter than that. You're like an old Hollywood starlet. I mean, you know, Old Hollywood. You're like a young, stunning Greta Garbo."

"You can't speak properly, poor man." I pretended to show sympathy.

It was so fun to tease him this way and how could I not be flattered? I happened to be the biggest Greta Garbo fan of all time. I had read everything there was to know about her and I'd even had pictures of her up in my first apartment, but that was a long time ago. That was the time Monique was nostalgic for, when we went shopping and did our makeup together in the years before grad school. And now it was back. I was achieving everything I'd wanted—a brilliant career and a man who could convince me I was as sexy as Greta Garbo. Wow.

I writhed on his lap and put my hands behind my head doing my best pin-up pose, while I made some of the sultriest facial expressions I could remember from those Old Hollywood posters. He watched me intently.

I leaned in and kissed him again, and he kissed me back so hard he almost bit me. He forced his tongue into my mouth aggressively, silently telling me he was taking charge now. I loved it when he used a bit of vigor. Then he held onto me, grabbing my bottom in his hands and he stood up, taking me with him. I'd always wanted a man to hold me this way. I wrapped my legs around his waist. Supporting myself with a firm grasp of his neck and shoulders, I laughed as I remembered Greta did in *Ninotchka*, with an effortlessness that was so natural. It was easy to laugh, easy to take pleasure in the decadence of this new reality.

He carried me over to the stereo system, which looked very high-tech. I'd have to study it later. He turned it on and immediately the room filled with sensual bossa nova music. It was dark outside and I was suddenly aware that all my new neighbors could see in because there were no curtains.

"Sebastian," I said. "We should either turn out the light or get out of the view."

"You don't want them to see what a slut you are?"

That got me so wet. I loved it when he talked dirty to me. I purred with delight into his ear but my good girl, polite side was too self-conscious. "I mean it, Sebastian. I feel weird about the whole city seeing me like this."

"Well then you won't like this at all," he said as he undid the hook of my bra. I clung to him, loving every second of this sexy man holding me like this. I especially responded to the feel of his hand down my naked back now that my bra was unclasped. But I yelped helplessly.

"You won't like this, either." He pulled the bra off completely so that my whole upper body was exposed. No one could see my breasts, of course, as they were turned in toward his chest.

"Sebastian! Stop teasing me."

"Oh, don't like getting a dose of your own medicine, I see," he said.

He switched his weight so he was only holding me with his right arm. He walked over to the wall by the door with me still clinging to him. When he pushed a button, the blinds slowly began to make their way across the window. He kissed me on my breasts and with his hand cupped my breast in his palm and held it up to his mouth and sucked my nipple. I almost came just at the sight and thought of it. All those strangers out there and the glimpse they got into my slutty reality. Oh my God. He'd made an exhibitionist out of me. That was the exact opposite of the old Claudia but the new Claudia had a very, very wet pussy.

"Mmm," I moaned and arched my back to give him better access to my breasts.

He bit down very gently. It drove me wild. There was an immediate response in my clit as he sucked and nibbled. Then he readjusted, held me with both hands and took the other nipple into his mouth. I was beside myself. My nipples were hard, and I remembered just how incredible an orgasm he'd given me at The Fairmont, and I was ready to come again. I couldn't help it. Like I did to him, he brought out the sex maniac in me. It was a side of myself that I had no control over. I was an animal around him.

"Fuck me," I said.

"What?"

"You heard me."

"What about…"

"Sebastian Porter, I want your cock in me and I can't wait any longer." Where had those words come from? Probably straight from my hungry clit, I chuckled to myself.

"Are you sure?"

Then, momentarily able to access my brainpower, I thought about the potential consequences. Deb had given her blessing, right? Sure, I'd feel weird meeting her knowing we had taken our relationship to the next level already. I wanted to be respectful, but she was in

Spain. In Spain! And I *couldn't* wait any longer. My cunt wouldn't let me. I was out of control. My pussy was doing all the thinking.

"I'm sure," I said. "Do you have protection?"

"I had a vasectomy," he said. "And my doctor ran all the STD tests on me as part of my regular check-up last time I was in."

"I thought you said you hadn't completely closed off the possibility of children," I said.

"They're reversible," he responded. "And anyway, I think I had closed myself off to all kinds of possibilities until I met you."

He approached me slowly, and caressed my face, brushing softly against my lower lip with his thumb. Time stopped for me in that moment. This was so much deeper than our bodies coming together. This was love. I kissed the palm of his hand.

"I want you on every level I can have you," I admitted.

He swept some loose strands of hair from my face then tucked them behind my ear. Gingerly, he traced the length of it down to the lobe, which gave me tingles everywhere.

"I'm clean, too," I whispered. "I'm on the pill. Have been for years. And I got checked out a month ago. Just a routine check-up, too." My mind fixated on the vasectomy news. "Are you telling me we don't need to use condoms?" I asked.

"That's what it sounds like to me."

"Oh my God," I gasped. I was gleeful in a way I couldn't hide.

"Does that turn you on?" he asked.

I nodded. "You have no idea."

"Have you ever had sex without condoms?"

I shook my head. "Never."

"Wow," he said. "That's pretty remarkable considering just how slutty you are."

"I know," I teased. "It is surprising considering how much I love cock." I couldn't believe the words coming out of my mouth. "Your cock, that is."

He rubbed himself against me. "Can you feel my cock right now? You're making me very hard with all your teasing."

"Mmm," I moaned. How I'd missed out on this form of verbal aphrodisiac all these years was beyond me. "Do you want to feel how wet my pussy is?"

"More than anything."

"Take me to the bedroom, Sebastian. I want you."

With that, he carried me to where my bed was miraculously already made and the duvet was gorgeous. It was white with a black swirly pattern on it, like paisley but different. Sebastian literally tossed me down, laughing at just how wild we were being. He came toward me, like a wolf, and put his hands right up my skirt. He grabbed onto my panty hose and underwear at the same time and gave a hard tug until my bum was exposed.

I reacted to his ferocity with a flirtatious biting of my lower lip. He pulled everything off me so all I wore was my gray pencil skirt. So I struggled with my hands behind me and undid the zipper in the back. As soon as the zipper was down, Sebastian tore the skirt off me so I was completely naked. What a sight this was with him perfectly clothed and me perfectly nude. I felt very, very slutty. It was liberating. All the years of being a good girl, of doing the right thing, of having a good head on my shoulders. I was ready for rebellion. I wanted nothing more than to access my inner sex goddess and let myself be free, truly free, with my kindred spirit, my sexy libertine boyfriend.

I sat up and reached for the top of his pants. I wanted to untuck his shirt and take it off but he stopped me.

"Get on your back where you belong," he ordered. "Put your head on the pillows."

I did as he'd said. I loved it when he told me what to do. Nothing could turn me on more. I never would have thought I had a submissive streak but here it was, and I was so ready to let myself embrace it. He climbed on top so that he sat between my legs. He gently took hold of a leg in each hand and pried them apart, not that I wasn't gladly spreading them for him.

"Ever since Calgary, I've been thinking about your sweet, delicious pussy."

"You have?"

"Your cunt drives me wild," he said and then he bent down and took a deep breath like he was smelling flowers in a meadow.

It was so exaggerated I almost wanted to laugh but it turned me on so much to think that my scent did this to him. He shook his head as though he couldn't believe it. Then he touched me with his forefinger.

"Claudia, you are positively soaking, you dirty girl."

"I am a dirty girl," I said. "It's true."

With one abrupt gesture, he put his finger into me. I gasped. Then he pulled it out and teased the opening of my pussy, getting his finger wet with me. He lifted it to his mouth and licked it clean. It was such a sexy sight. He did it again, this time running two of his fingers across my pussy, like he was covertly dipping them into a jar of honey. He lifted them up to his mouth then sucked them clean.

"Mmm," he said. "I love the way you taste. I could live on eating your pussy."

Again he returned his fingers to my cunt and covered them in my juices. This time he stuck both fingers inside me, fucking me gently like that. I moaned in delight. Then he took them out and slowly, like he wanted me to taste this delicious honey, he put his fingers in my mouth. I tasted myself — sweet and salty. It blew my mind to think of myself as a delicacy to be savored. How did he manage to make me feel so sexy?

"Mmm," I said.

He smiled as though he'd just let me in on the best-kept secret in the world.

He turned me on so much with the way he took pleasure in my body. He brought out the goddess that had been long dormant. With my foot hooked behind Sebastian's head, I lowered him, directing him straight to my awaiting pussy. He licked me all over, exploring me with his tongue as he proceeded to give me the same kind of all-encompassing oral sex he'd showed me he was capable of last time. He seemed to lose himself completely, as though he was in another world. I saw a pleasure machine that existed just for me.

I could let him do it to me like that forever. He didn't seem to get tired. It was incredible. I wondered how he could consider himself old with skills and stamina like that. At the same time, I loved the sight of his graying hair. I loved that he was older. It made me feel really naughty. I was living out a schoolgirl fantasy, something totally taboo to me. I'd seen couples out and about in the past who had a visible age difference and it always seemed like lecherous old men preying on hot young things that didn't know any better. I hadn't seen what was in it for the girl, not until I'd experienced it myself. There was something about being the not-so-naïve coquette. And the fact that he had set me up exactly the way he wanted me drove me wild.

It was weird how it affected me, how it turned me on to think about the eyes of the world watching. I thought about the judgments. *He looks old enough to be her father.* And instead of being offensive, in this moment, those perceptions seemed so titillating. I guess it was my own way of decontextualizing, of making it okay, but it wasn't defensive. It was amazing. To me there was a natural attraction between younger women and older men based on maturity. If it were true that girls matured faster than boys, then why not go for an older guy? It was clear to me that Sebastian had made mistakes that he'd learned from. Guys my age were still out there making mistakes. And Sebastian was so passionate sexually. It was as though the taboo nature of our connection turned us both on so much that it brought out his animalism. It was predatory by nature.

It brought me back to all my old fantasies. Mr Josard, my French teacher on whom I had the biggest crush for all of my high school years. And then the professors I met later on during my undergraduate degree, how they turned me on with their minds and experience. It was a wonder I hadn't tried this out before. It seemed a natural fit. I let myself relax totally under Sebastian's tongue. He divided his attention fairly all over, passing my clit every so often to remind me that if he wanted he could make me come right then. Meanwhile, I studied him. I took in the sexy image in front of me — my own legs, spread apart — how slutty I looked — and his large frame hulking over me. The sounds he made drove me wild. Now and then he sucked my clit gently into his mouth, creating the most amazing vacuum sensation and threatening to make me burst and release all the tension that was building.

He reached up and squeezed my nipples with both hands. Then he paused and stared at me, his mouth glistening. He licked his lips.

"I want you to taste how good you are," he said and lay down on top of me, before kissing me hard.

Tasting my own flavor delivered by the pressure of his confident tongue drove me into sheer bliss. It was as though we were engaged in a dance of the mouth, both of us exploring the other, pushing and pulling, teasing and revealing.

He pulled back so he could take my nipple into his mouth, causing me to writhe and moan.

"Mmm," I said, pressing my pelvis into the bed as my pussy throbbed and demanded attention. "I really need you to fuck me."

"Patience, my slut. You'll get fucked. Trust me."

"You're torturing me."

He nodded. "Two can play at your game. And it is a fun game to play, isn't it?"

"Uh huh," I agreed.

I'd have agreed to anything at that moment. With the bossa nova music coming from the other room, we were in a completely new world, a place I'd never been before, a fantasy land wherein everything felt incredibly sensual. My skin was so receptive to his touch.

"I love these sexy nipples," he said, sitting up so he could admire them. "Look at them. How can you stand being so perfect?"

He cupped my breasts and massaged them, exposing just the nipples on each breast. It felt like he wanted to hold every part of me and I loved it. Then he surprised me by flicking my right nipple, the way one might flick a crumb off a table. It stung slightly and sent a direct shock to my clit. He watched me closely.

"You liked that, didn't you?"

I nodded.

"I could tell you needed a little disciplining." His face was suddenly stern. Then he flicked the other nipple. Both of them hardened in response to his harshness. "Look how they're standing in attention," he said, pleased with himself.

I felt such urgency in my cunt—I'd go out of my mind if he didn't fuck me soon. He was terrible. How could he torture me this way? Oh, how I loved it.

"Get up," he ordered.

What? Wasn't he going to fuck me?

He rolled me onto my side and I found myself in a kneeling position at the foot end of the bed, delirious and confused. Then he lay down where I had been and beckoned me with his hands, motioning for me to come to him. I did.

"I want you to sit on my face," he divulged. He was so forceful in stating his desires.

It was something I both admired and was aroused by. I was so hungry for his cock I wanted nothing more than to climb on top of him and put his now huge and gorgeous cock in me. But I dared not do anything but what he said. He was controlling this game, leading me, like it was the tango. The music from the other room still had its effect.

So I crawled up to him. When I was adjacent to his shoulders, facing him, I placed my right leg over him, straddling his face. Slowly, very slowly—because I'd never been in this position before—I lowered myself onto him. His tongue was surprisingly hard. He was sticking it out and it was like sinking onto a stiff cock when he slipped it into me. I had not been expecting that. He held me by my hips and he was bench pressing me, pushing me up and letting me come back down gradually, as he would a barbell weight. It was so hot the way he was controlling my movements even though I was the one sitting on his face.

His moans were muffled. I turned around to look behind me and his cock was so hard it was standing perfectly erect, perfectly ready for me, but I could tell he wasn't going to let me have it.

Instead, he fucked me with his tongue and he fucked hard. When he took it out and flicked my clit with it, I was so turned on I couldn't handle it anymore.

"I think I'm going to come if you keep licking me like that," I said.

All he said was, "Mmm."

He kept on torturing my clit with the surface of his tongue, rubbing it in complete circles, like we were twirling on the dance floor. My clit was so hard and demanded release under his touch. I writhed and fucked his face. This position had always seemed too strange to me. How could I climb on top of my lover and fuck him, rub myself all over him then come in his mouth? It seemed so dirty I'd never even tried it. *What foolishness!* I loved the idea of coming in Sebastian's mouth and letting him taste me. He was obviously into it as he'd been the one to put me here so I went for it. I let myself go. I rocked back and forth on his mouth for a while, stroking myself with his soft tongue, and then I needed more pressure so I went at his mouth a little harder and found that perfect rhythm.

"I'm going to come so hard," I said.

He extended his hand behind me and, without looking, I could tell from his new movements that he was stroking his cock. The thought of it turned me on immensely. He couldn't handle the pressure either. So I fucked his face even harder, bucking down against his tongue that he kept stiff for my pleasure. Suddenly, my pussy contracted and spasmed. I was releasing right onto him and the thought of it filled me with so much mind-blowing pleasure that I came harder than ever before. He seemed to savor every second of it, like he'd been thirsting in the desert and was desperate to suck up every drop from my pussy. He moaned with delight, then forgetting about his cock again he took my hips between his palms and held me down on him. As my body melted into relaxation, I held onto my new headboard and let out a massive moan.

When it was over, I laid down beside him, totally spent. My body was limp from the release and he turned on his side and stroked my skin with his hand even though his cock was so hard, it was threatening to burst against my thigh.

I couldn't help but take his cock in my hand. It was the only intuitive thing to do, to hold his hardness and grip him, but he slapped my hand away. It was as though he'd made up his mind that I was not going to get to pleasure him. Or maybe he had some rules about what constituted fucking and I didn't know about them.

"Not yet," he said.

His restraint was unbelievable. He'd made me come a couple of times but he wasn't going to let me reciprocate. This was very strange male behavior.

"Don't you need release?" I asked.

He nodded. "Badly."

"Let me help you."

His demeanor changed completely and now it was like he just wanted us to cuddle. He took me in his arms and held me tight.

"Come with me," he ordered.

He took me by the hand and led me to the large bathroom down the hall. I wanted to protest and pull him back so I could give him the kind of pleasure he gave me.

"Wait. What about you?"

"Claudia, sweet woman. Do you have any idea how much you turn me on?"

I was dizzy after such an intense orgasm. "It's mutual, my sex god."

In the bathroom, he turned on the water and sat on the edge of the Jacuzzi tub testing the temperature with his hand.

"I hope you don't mind that I want us to wait a while longer before penetrative sex."

He sounded so funny saying that, using such clinical terminology to describe the magnetism between us.

"I don't mind," I said. "Even though it is torturous."

"Delayed gratification," he continued. "It's healthy."

He pulled me in close and kissed me. I wanted to get lost in those lips forever. There was so much to figure out about him but when our lips met, I could tell that everything about this was right. The body knows. My body was definitely comfortable around his.

"You make me happy," I said.

Chapter Eight

Time passed quickly. We couldn't see much of each other during the week as I had several department meetings and had to write out lesson plans in case I was called in for an interview. It was good that I'd heard that rumor. I could at least be ready.

On top of that, I had to get settled in my new place. Sebastian told me that no matter what happened between him and me, there was a one-year lease on the apartment. I could live there rent-free the entire time, so there was nothing to lose and I finally recognized it as a generous offering with no strings attached.

Monique came over.

"Shut up. Shut up. Shut up," she said over and over as she examined all the nooks and crannies of the place. She loved the view, the décor, the incredible bathrooms, and she found storage space I hadn't even noticed before as well as lighting built into the bookcases in my office and heating in the floor tiles in the kitchen and bathroom.

"This is the Taj Mahal of apartments," she concluded. "And look!" she said, opening two cupboards in the kitchen, "you've got an espresso machine! And there's even a slot where your coffee grounds go. They fall into your apartment composter. This place is insane!"

"Yeah." I nodded. "Pretty great." And my sweetheart loved me enough to make sure I was in a safe building. The neighborhood was not too far from my previous one so I still saw a number of familiar faces. Most importantly, I felt protected and loved even when I wasn't in Sebastian's presence and I realized that's precisely how he wanted me to feel.

"Thanks for helping me get settled," I said as I fetched a bottle of shiraz from the rack and uncorked it for us. There were glasses in the cupboards already. None of my old life had infringed on the luxury.

Monique sighed, lost in her own little world as she gazed at the glass in her hand. "How come I can't have a perfect boyfriend who treats me so well?"

"How are things with Jerome?" I knew that was what she wanted to talk about.

She sighed again. "Okay, I guess. I mean, stupid. He and I were in the elevator together on Thursday. It was just the two of us, but he just stood there and asked how I liked working for Hugh and complimented me on my skills at work and said his new assistant wasn't as competent. Blah blah blah."

Monique even gave hand signals as though she was holding a puppet. The way she imitated him when she didn't like what he did was so hilarious, but I didn't dare say anything or she'd become self-conscious about it and stop.

"Well, he's your ex-boss. It seems like a perfectly reasonable way to talk to you in my opinion."

She huffed. "In the past, when we took the elevator together, there was so much tension between us I sometimes wondered which one of us would break down and push the Emergency Stop button."

"Well, you work together. It's probably best not to have that anyway."

"Whatever," she said brazenly. "Look at you and Sebastian. Besides, show me one work place where people aren't trying to get into each other's pants."

"Um, let's see," I was up for the challenge. "Midwifery?" I was just having fun with her. I didn't know anything about the world of midwives.

"That's almost exclusively women and I think lots of midwives are lesbians so for sure some are partnered with other midwives so that just proves my point," she said. "People hook up at work. It's totally normal. It happens all the time and in every industry. Look at that CIA dude in the news and his biographer. It's bound to happen especially when people work closely together."

"Well, still. I don't think it's wrong of Jerome to keep it professional since you have to work together."

"Whose side are you on?" She smirked.

"I'm just saying, I get what he's doing but you don't know how he feels outside of work. Maybe he gave you some space so that he could ask you out later."

"That makes no sense. He's over me. He had the hots for me for a while, then he got over it and had me transferred. He discarded me."

"Don't say that."

"It's the truth."

"I doubt that."

"Fuck him," she said, signaling the end of the conversation.

Monique had always been able to do end things on a sour note of betrayal or anguish then move on. Even though she'd been pining for Jerome for a couple of years now, if she said 'fuck him', she was somewhere on the path to recovery. By next week, she'd be splurging on a day at the spa and soon enough there'd be another guy. She was strong that way.

What struck me as very odd was the way things had turned around between us. She'd always been the glamour girl with crushes on hot guys who took her to fancy places and bought her nice stuff. She had a whole drawer of jewelry from previous boyfriends, potential boyfriends and guys who weren't potentials but whom she toyed with. She had received handbags, shoes, weekend getaways and sexy text messages. Everything. And I'd always been the boring one in jeans and a turtleneck, with the same old boring and broke boyfriend who had stopped trying to be romantic a long time ago. It was so strange to be the one with news, the one with stuff to show and stories to tell. I didn't want to make too big a deal of everything but I also didn't know how to downplay my Taj Mahal, expensive gifts and sudden state of abundance. So maybe I'd do what she had done with me so many times and share the wealth. I could afford it now, after all.

"You know what we need?"

"What?"

"A night out on the town."

"I don't know. I'm not exactly up for that."

"Come on. You can borrow something of mine. Let me take you out for once. You're the best friend I've ever had."

"Really?"

I noticed she was teary and realized she'd always been the big sister in our friendship. This time it was up to me to help her feel better.

"Yeah, come on. I think I have a Max Azria dress that would fit you perfectly."

"Whoa," she said. "There's something I never expected to hear from you."

I smiled. "It's clingy material. It'll be gorgeous on you."

We raided my closet and makeup collection. She was radiant in my dress, and I couldn't believe I had something she wanted to wear. I also wore a dress and we had both made our eyes dramatically dark. This was a real girls' night out.

When we got to Orion's, the trendy cocktail lounge Monique had suggested, I could see why this place had suddenly become the place all the food blogs raved about. It was packed with sexy, seemingly eligible men. We were near the downtown core, close to the law courts and the business district. The men were mostly in suits or business casual attire. This was not a place I would have even walked into a few months ago, even if I had been with Monique. The place just oozed upward mobility, expensive watches and cars, and guys looking for arm candy wives. It was perfect for tonight's goal—getting Monique's mind off Jerome.

We were seated at a little corner table. Monique had once told me that was a major compliment to be seated near the window like we were. It meant that the servers deemed us hot. I definitely felt hot that night.

We ordered martinis and appetizers, and before long, Monique's good looks had reeled in a couple of hunky guys. The two approached our table, which conveniently had space enough for four.

"Are you expecting anyone?" one asked.

"Or can we join you?" asked the other.

"Please." Monique gestured at the seats next to us.

I could tell she already had her sights on the first guy. She looked intently at him, and I suspected he had no idea what he was in for. When they introduced themselves, we learned that the guy Monique liked was named Troy. The other one was Patrick. Patrick and I understood from the start what our role in this whole game was. We were cordial with each other and made conversation, but it was clear that the real attraction this evening was between Monique and Troy. Monique touched his arm, thereby opening the floodgates of bodily contact. After that, Troy found all sorts of excuses to move in on her, punctuating his stories with gestures that subtly encroached on her until they were sitting so close he might as well have taken her on his lap.

I was sipping sparkling water. I'd switched after the second martini, unlike Monique who was on her fourth. This was one of those situations they turn into a Lifetime Movie of the Week where a sexy drunk girl makes a big mistake and winds up on a sex tape all over the Internet. I was not about to let that happen, so I turned into her chaperone and made sure she didn't go home with Troy. He already had his arm around her and his hand on her lap and she loved every second of it.

Call me cautious but I didn't like the idea of her hooking up with someone we'd only just met, especially when her heart was hurting over Jerome and she was not exactly of sober mind.

"We should probably get going, eh, Monique?" I started gesturing toward the door.

"The fun has just begun," Troy said.

"Yeah," Monique agreed. "I'm having a great time."

"I'm having fun, too," Patrick said, giving me a glance that suggested he was hoping to keep the night going.

I had no experience in getting rid of guys. This was one department I'd never had to deal with so I just sat there for a while, outnumbered, drinking sparkling water, trying to figure out a plan while Monique and Troy made out right in front of me and Patrick. It was awkward, to say the least.

I tried again. "Okay, well I think I best be going."

Monique took her tongue out of Troy's mouth and looked at me like I was being bothersome, interrupting her personal Seven Minutes in Heaven game.

"Already?" Monique whined.

This was just like high school. Getting her to go home back then had also been a total nightmare, especially if she'd been making out with a cute guy. But this was no longer high school and I didn't want my best friend out with this dude who might not even have given us his real name.

"Come on, Monique. We're going. It was lovely to meet both of you," I said, wrangling my best friend free of the handsome stranger she was attached to.

She made sure to get Troy's phone number by having him call her phone. It appeared he had not lied about his name, but nevertheless, I was ready to call it quits on girls' night. We took a cab back to my apartment. She fell asleep on the way.

I hauled her up on the elevator with my arm wrapped around her waist.

"That was fun," Monique said, sounding slightly more sober. She kicked her heels off at the front door and walked to the kitchen. "Got anything to eat?"

I followed her, opened my fridge and took out some eggs. On the counter I had a loaf of bread. "I'll make you an egg in a nest," I said, taking a shot glass from the cupboard to cut a perfectly round hole in the center of the bread. I began buttering.

Monique propped herself up on the counter and watched. "Can you believe those two?" she asked.

"Yeah," I said. "Crazy."

"But it was fun going out," she said, looking off into the distance as I got out the frying pan and put the two pieces of buttered bread in it.

"Yeah," I said. "It was like the good old days."

"We're fabulous," she said.

"We are." I cracked an egg into each hole and shook a bit of salt onto the nests. There was nothing quite as comforting as this. It was a real house warming moment.

When the nests were ready, I put them on plates. We went back into the living room and sunk into the couches to take satisfying bites of the late night snack. I missed Sebastian. It was a strange feeling to have had a night like this.

"Stay over," I told Monique. "Sleep in my bed. It's too late for you to go home and I've got plenty of room."

"I thought you'd never ask," she said, finishing her snack and putting the plate on the coffee table. She got up and walked to the bedroom.

I followed.

I gave her a T-shirt to wear and changed into my pajamas. By the time I'd turned off the light and crawled into bed, she was already sleeping soundly.

Chapter Nine

As I fumbled about with garlic and butter in my effort to seduce Sebastian with Seafood Alfredo, he opened a bottle of chardonnay and got two glasses from the cupboard. He came up behind me as I was chopping garlic and put his hands around my waist. He kissed my cheek.

"A toast to us," he said, passing me a glass. "I feel so fortunate to have you in my life."

"Me too."

We toasted then went over to the dinner table to light the candles.

He told me he'd gone back into his studio and had had a long meditation about his artistic practice and process. I listened but was also busy getting dinner ready and timing everything just so. It was great to hear that he was doing it again and he made a big point of telling me how much I'd inspired him, which was flattering since I felt like it was the other way around. I got him to sit down at the table and served him the dish. I had fresh parmesan from the Italian deli around the corner. He marveled at his plate and offered a lot of *ooohs* and *aaahs*.

"This is incredible," he said as he tried the first bite. "I can't believe you made this."

I shrugged and did my best to seem meek. Of course I had done everything I could to make the meal as good as could be. I'd even gone across town to the best seafood dealer for the scallops and prawns. He was so animated in his enjoyment of the pasta dish that we talked about it for a long time.

"Sebastian?"

"Yes?"

"I fantasize about your cock all the time."

He choked on a mouthful of pasta, which he nearly had to spit into his napkin. He recovered, but my revelation must have caught him off guard. "You do?"

I took a sip of wine and swallowed. "I want you to claim me."

"Claim you?"

"Yes."

"What on earth do you mean?"

"I mean, I want you to make me yours."

"Claudia, how utterly 1950s of you."

"Sexually," I added. "Not socially."

"That's better. Now tell me more." He leaned in, curious, hanging on every word.

"When we're together, I long for your cock. I want you to turn me into your plaything and all I can think about is pleasing you."

"I had no idea you had such a submissive streak, you naughty girl."

"I didn't either."

"I've never wanted to be in control this much before. I guess you bring that out in me."

"How so?"

"You just do. I can't explain it. I want to fuck you badly. Really badly. More than you know. But somehow, controlling it, making you wait—making me wait—is an incredible turn on for me."

I bit my lip. I could almost feel myself drooling. "How much longer are you going to make me wait?"

"I was going to make love to you tonight."

"Make love?" I snickered. "Is that what we're calling it?"

"Isn't it?"

"Sebastian, we're way more perverted than that. Good people make love. When we're between the sheets, I wouldn't exactly call us saints."

"So that good girl image I have of you…"

"Totally false."

"I see." He smiled. "Then I want to fuck you tonight."

My pussy throbbed. I was ready for him to clear the table by shoving everything to one side like they do in the movies and lift me onto it. I wanted him to take me right there.

"Oh, Sebastian. You know exactly how to talk to me."

"I do?"

I nodded. "You've got all the moves."

"Come here," he said, standing up. "Get in that bedroom."

He blew out the candles. Then he patted my bum again. How I loved his palm on my bottom. More than I dared admit.

We got into the bedroom and he sat down on the bed.

"Wait here," I said.

"You're going to leave me here? All turned on? How can you do that? You cruel woman."

I smiled. "I'll be right back. It'll be worth the wait."

I went into the bathroom where I'd already laid out a provocative, cupless bodice. There was no fabric to cover up my breasts. Though I was in black lace, my breasts were perfectly exposed, just how I liked them.

The previous afternoon I'd gotten myself waxed, something I'd stopped doing around the same time I moved in with Pete. It had seemed imperative to get it done again, to connect with the bad girl side of myself that had lain dormant for way too long.

I couldn't help but touch myself. The smoothness of my skin beckoned. It made perfect sense to me that women would get this done in spite of the pain. It heightened all sensation so when I pulled on the G-string panties that came with the bodice, I couldn't help but indulge the sensation of lace against sensitive skin by fingering myself a little. Divine.

I emerged from the bathroom a bona fide bad girl. I was ready to feel Sebastian inside me. I wanted nothing more.

When he saw me, his eyes told me everything I needed to know.

"Come here," he ordered.

I swooned at how he talked, how he commanded. Maybe that was the good girl in me. I wanted to please. I wanted to do as he said. And in doing what he said, I'd have exactly what I wanted. He took my breasts in his hands.

"You are so hot," he said. Then, as he held my breast in his left hand, he gave my nipple a smack with his right. It sent an immediate message to my waiting clit.

"Naughty girl."

"Mmm. Yeah." I loved it when he called me that. It made me so wet.

He did the same to the other breast, giving me a hard smack right on my nipple. It stung in the best possible way.

"You like that, don't you?"

I nodded.

He got up and tossed me onto the bed. "On your knees."

"Okay."

He controlled my movements with his hands and made sure to position my butt in his direction. I moved it around, a little to tease him.

"Come here, my slut. Let me take these off." He pulled on the sides of my panties. I knew they wouldn't last long. And then I heard him gasp when their removal revealed smooth skin beneath.

"You didn't. You little slut." He ran his forefinger over my labia which was by now completely soaked.

"I did," I said. "Do you like it?"

"I love it."

"I thought you might."

Without hesitation, he entered me with his finger. I let out a gasp because I was actually shocked by the immediacy. He fucked me like that for several minutes. With his other hand, he reached around and tweaked my nipples, trying to hold onto both of my dangling breasts with one hand. His palm was large but not that large. Then he patted my bum.

"I can't wait any longer," he said. He unzipped his pants.

I craned my neck to watch him as his pants dropped to the floor and he stepped out of them. He took his boxers off along with his socks, shirt and undershirt. He tossed each piece of his clothing on the floor. His cock was already hard and pointed straight at my cunt. Was he going to shove it in as recklessly and eagerly as he'd done with his finger, I wondered.

"Come here," he said. "Take me between your gorgeous lips.

I thought he'd never ask. *Gladly!*

I sat down on the edge of the bed and with him standing, I was the exact height to engulf his cock. It was so good to finally do this. I'd wanted to for so long. So long. Looking up at him, I was turned on by the way he leaned his head back and let out a moan. It was the ideal vision to go along with the knowledge that I was his plaything. I closed my eyes and found the perfect rhythm, moving my mouth up and down his stiff cock. Then I opened my eyes to find him watching me closely. It was like he couldn't believe his eyes. I couldn't exactly smile but I smiled with my eyes and he moaned in response.

He took my face in his hands and held onto me as he fucked my mouth. He was so hard and he had control as he pumped in and out. I loved giving oral sex partly because of the tension between us, the anticipation that had built up for so long. Plus, I loved surrendering to him, submitting to his desires and he knew it. He could tell, I was sure, just from the way I relaxed my jaw and cradled his cock on my tongue, creating a bed for his cock to rest on. He was slow in his thrusting. I could have kept him in that position all night, like I wanted him to fuck my mouth until he couldn't take it anymore. Sebastian must have sensed that I was willing to suck him until he ejaculated because he withdrew his cock, much to my disappointment, until I considered the adventure ahead.

"Get on your back, woman."

I tossed myself backwards and squirmed my way up to the headboard. He climbed on top of me and kissed my décolletage.

"Are you ready for me?"

I'd been ready for a long time. "Yes, oh, yes."

"Tell me what you want."

Oh, Sebastian. He knew just how to challenge me. If there was one thing I had not yet learned it was how to ask for what I wanted with force and command, especially where sex was concerned. Having been a good girl all my life, these past few weeks of letting my bad girl out with him were not enough to unleash the truly insatiable monster I had inside me. Why did he torture me? I tried to beckon him with my eyes but it was no use. I knew he wasn't going to fuck me until I asked for it.

I took a deep breath. "Sebastian, I want your cock in me. I need you to fuck me."

"That's a good girl," he said as he meticulously placed his cock right at my opening.

He semi-kneeled, enough to give himself the height required to watch every second of his cock slipping slowly and carefully into my wet cunt. My pussy was being stretched to accommodate his girth. He was huge.

"Oh, yeah," I cried. "Like that. I want your dick to fill me up."

He leaned forward, his cock buried inside me, and caressed my hair as he pushed himself deeper. "I've been waiting for you to say that," he whispered.

"I want you to fuck me, Sebastian. I love the feeling of your cock in my pussy." I was ready to let go of my inhibitions completely, ready to surrender to my ultimate fantasies of being his dirty little slut.

"That's it, baby."

"Mmm," I moaned. "Make me your fuck toy."

His cock was so hard and long that his thrusts provided a combination of pain and pleasure that threatened to make me faint from overload. It was the thought of it, the feel of it, all of it that made me so incredibly aroused I could barely control myself. He fucked me like that for a few minutes, my mind stretching itself, like my pussy was, to accommodate the thought of him.

He stopped. He pulled out and gestured for me to come forward once more. My head was in his hands as he lifted me out of my missionary pose and brought me to my knees once more. He plunged his cock in my mouth. I could taste my pussy on his dick and it was delightful. He sat as I sucked his dick. Then he laid down where I had been and pulled me onto him. I loved being guided. I loved the way his hands instructed me, just like when we danced tango.

"Now fuck me," he said.

I straddled him. I skillfully lowered my cunt steadily and slid his dick into my pussy. He held onto my hips and entered me with such force that his butt left the mattress. Our bodies made a loud smacking sound between us.

"I love feeling your cock in me," I said.

"Good, baby," he said, "because I love watching you ride me. You know what you're doing."

I channeled my inner temptress. I closed my eyes and concentrated only on my own pleasure. It was my turn to have exactly what I wanted. I fucked him slowly, allowing his cock to massage me. I moaned and tossed my head back, my hair cascading around my shoulders. My skin was hyper sensitive, so my hair tickled my back and took me to ecstatic heights. Lust took over completely and I rode him like a cowgirl. I was following the elusive orgasm that beckoned. I had to have it. I wanted nothing more than release. I leaned forward so that my clit rubbed against the top of his cock, giving me control. That pushed me over the edge. In pure abandon, I let myself come being loud, sweaty and unabashedly sexual.

Sebastian's hands held me still as my pussy gripped him. He pushed into the pulsating sensations and released, emitting a final agonized moan. We stayed connected for what seemed like eternity in perfect union. I lay prostrate on his chest, listening to the pounding of his heart and savoring the spasms and contractions of our bodies relinquishing themselves to each other. Our energies commingled and I knew I would never be the same again, for I could no longer think of us as separate. This moment of sweet togetherness would stay with me even when we were apart.

Afterward, I flopped down beside him then yawned and closed my eyes as I pulled his arms around me. He held me, stroking my hair and making me tingle all over. He kissed the top of my head as I closed my eyes and enjoyed the moment. I fell asleep like that.

* * * *

The next morning, I woke up to the aroma of coffee. I got up and followed the smell just like characters in cartoons did, all the way to the espresso machine in the kitchen that Sebastian was busy operating.

"Good morning," he said, already chipper. It looked like he was on his second cup.

I grumbled, still sleepy from our very athletic night together. He came over to me and held me close. I felt so safe and warm in his arms, a feeling I didn't want to let go of.

I was enjoying my espresso and silently scanning the newspaper headlines when Sebastian leaned down and kissed the top of my head. It was an intimate gesture that punctuated the morning.

We spent the remainder of the day lazing about my apartment, before going out for groceries. I bought everything that I needed to make lasagna, and Sebastian insisted on carrying my grocery bags. I let him. I also let him buy a bottle of wine that, even now, I could not get myself to buy. It was one thing to have money, it was another to adjust to the lifestyle of it.

Back in the kitchen, while I was prepping the ingredients, Sebastian said, "Deb and Hatia asked me to ask you to dinner next Saturday."

I had butterflies. Everything felt strange. It was the overwhelming sense that things would inevitably change, and I wasn't sure I wanted them to. I had finally found the man I'd subconsciously been looking for all along and we had only just taken our relationship to the next level.

"Okay," I said, in spite of my anxiety about it.

He stood beside me and tilted my face toward his, guiding me with the fingers he placed beneath my chin. Our eyes met.

"You will like them. I promise."

"What if I don't? Or worse, what if they don't like me?"

"They will," he persisted.

If I lost Sebastian, I'd be devastated. It was a hard thing to recognize because we were so new but it was there—the dream that we could be together. So I couldn't help but feel a little delusional since he had already lived that dream with Deb. He had a family unit with her and who was I in comparison to all that? Where did I fit in?

I pulled back from him.

"What's the matter?"

"I just don't want to lose you," I said. "I guess I don't like the powerlessness I feel right now."

"I understand." He tried to take me in his arms, but I put my hands on his chest in protest.

"Well, yeah," I scoffed. "This could all disappear if Deb decides she doesn't like me."

"But she wouldn't make that choice." He put his hand on my back and made circular motions as though to comfort me. It was impossible to resist his touch.

I nodded. "Okay, well, if you say so." I was placated by his caresses.

"Claudia, you have to want this, too."

"I do."

"I don't want you putting up with my family because you feel obligated. I'd like us to all get along and respect each other."

"This is just so strange for me, Sebastian. Your daughter is only fourteen years younger than I am."

"I know. I get it."

"What if I freak out?"

"Do you think you'd freak out?"

"I might." I said it more to be flirtatious but I don't think it worked.

Sebastian looked worried. "How?"

"I'm scared I'm going to feel like your mistress or something."

He grabbed me and held me so tight I thought he'd squeeze all the air out of me. "You're not my mistress. You're my lover. Deb has her lover, too. This is how it works."

"Am I being silly in worrying?"

"No, you're being emotionally responsible, trying to anticipate how you will feel. It's very good that you're communicating that. Now that I know, I can behave accordingly. I want you two to meet. I want us to work. That's all."

I nodded. "I want us to work, too."

Chapter Ten

I was in my office that I share with two other TAs having my last office hour of the semester. No students came to see me since all the work was done and everyone was in holiday mode by then. I flipped through a scholarly text on Milton's influences and tried to pay attention. A knock sounded at the door and when I opened it, Paul was there.

"Hey," I said. "What's up?" He had never knocked on my door before.

"I was wondering if you heard the big news."

"What big news?" The only big news in my world was that I had the most important dinner party of my life to attend the next day and couldn't think about anything else.

"You got the position."

"What?"

"They announced it on the news bulletin."

"What? But they didn't even call me in for a formal interview."

After the last department meeting, a bunch of us had chatted, and the chair, along with a few of the tenured professors, had bantered with me. I thought it was all quite hypothetical, like they were testing me. They had asked about my availability and I'd given them the honest truth that this job was everything to me, that it had been hard to commit to the ascetic life of full-time studying and that I'd gone and gotten an additional job to supplement my income but that I was committed to the academy for the long haul. I guessed they'd liked what I had said. In spite of the informal setting, we'd also discussed classroom pedagogy and possible lesson plans. Still, if I'd got the job, they had to be the world's most chilled out hiring committee.

"So how come you know before me?" I asked. I was skeptical.

"They didn't call you?"

I shook my head.

"Have you checked messages?"

I checked my bag. In fact, I'd missed three calls from the department that morning. My ringer was off. *Oh my God. It might actually be true.* I couldn't fathom it. But I called the number. Paul stood in the door frame.

"Claudia," George said. "I've been calling you."

"Yeah, I just noticed the missed calls. Sorry."

"Don't be sorry. I have good news."

"Yeah?"

"The department would like you to teach your own course this fall."

"Oh my God. Really?" I sounded like a school girl but it was so unreal.

"Drop by my office on your way out and we'll discuss the details."

After I got off the phone, I hugged Paul.

"Holy shit!" I blurted. "I was not expecting that."

He nodded. "Hey, what are you doing? I'm going to the pub soon, if you want to join. I'd love to celebrate this with you."

"Sounds awesome. I'm supposed to stay until five but there's no way anyone's coming. Why don't I head over to George's office now and I'll see you at the pub?"

"Cool."

Before leaving the privacy of my dark little shared office, I called Sebastian.

"Wow," he said when I told him. "That is fantastic news. Congratulations."

"Thanks," I said. "I had to call you immediately. I'm so excited. I can hardly believe it."

"Claudia, get used to it. The world wants to see you shine."

"I can't wait to celebrate this with you. Maybe tonight?"

"Deb and Hatia are getting in and, well, I had planned to be around to receive them."

"Okay," I said, totally aware of my own disappointment. "Well, one of my friends in the department invited me to the pub so I'm going to go celebrate with him then."

"Sounds good. We'll see you tomorrow for dinner and we'll celebrate then."

"Yep," I said.

"I miss you," he whispered.

"You too," I said and ended the conversation there. *If he missed me that much, he'd find a way to see me when I had such important news.*

I headed to George's office, found out that I'd be paid quite handsomely. I asked George to join us at the pub but he said he was too old to hang out there.

* * * *

"To Claudia!" Paul raised a pint.

We had to shout to hear each other in the noisy student pub.

Between us, we shared a pitcher, and a couple of hours later, Paul asked me about my new look. He leaned in. I told him about falling for an older man. It felt good to say it out loud.

"Well, since we're being honest and clearing the air, I have to confess that I've had a little crush on you for quite some time."

"You have?"

He nodded. "Don't get weirded out. I am a gentleman."

I'd had no clue about this and somehow it made me feel like I wasn't nearly as mousy and dull as Monique had suggested.

"Well, it's an honor," I said. "You're a quality guy. I'm sure you'll find your match soon."

"You're pretty gaga over this Sebastian guy, eh?" Paul asked.

I wondered if he was fishing around to see if there was still a chance between us. It was impossible to wrap my mind around that concept. Yet there it was.

I nodded.

"Well, a guy can dream."

I was totally floored. Truth be told, I had always considered Paul out of my league. He was gorgeous and as sharp as a whip. Any girl would be lucky to date him.

* * * *

I'd been home all of twenty minutes, just enough time to get out of my work clothes and into my sweat pants and T-shirt, when the buzzer went off.

"Hello?" I assumed it was some misguided delivery person.

"It's Sebastian. Can I come up?"

"Yeah." I buzzed him in.

I answered the door and could barely see him for the floral bouquet that blocked my view of him. Behind a bush-sized amount of pink lilies and peonies, he was beaming at me.

"For you," he said. "Congratulations."

"Thank you." I wanted to cry. This was everything I'd wanted that I hadn't ever thought I'd get. I berated myself for doubting him earlier. "Come in. Don't mind my grubby clothes."

"You could never look grubby. In fact, you look hot as hell right now, Professor Richards."

"Oh my God. That's what they're going to be calling me next year." I gasped. I could not stop myself from jumping up and down. I was filled with energy. How had my life turned so amazing so quickly?

"You deserve it."

I took the bouquet into the living room and set it on the coffee table. It was huge, by a landslide the largest I'd ever received. "You didn't have to," I said.

"I wanted to."

"I thought it'd be hard for you to get away."

"When I told Deb about your promotion, she scolded me for not going to you right away."

"She did?" I was impressed. This boded very well indeed.

"Yeah, and I saw the error of my ways. Believe me. It's not every day that someone I care so much about receives such good news."

"Aww. Thanks."

"So I want us to celebrate."

"What about Deb and Hatia?"

"We're still on for tomorrow night. Let's spend tonight together celebrating your accomplishments."

Remarkable! "How did I suddenly get so lucky? All my dreams are coming true."

"Well, that's what happens to amazing people such as yourself. So, would you like to order in or go out?"

Overwhelmed with joy, I felt a tear fall down my cheek. It was great to be celebrated. "Let's go out."

"I know the perfect place," Sebastian said.

"Me too. And it's my treat. My promotion."

"No, I insist. Let's go to the Shangri-La. You will love their cocktails and they also have an amazing lobster bisque."

"Sorry, Sebastian. It's my night and I want to go to Tony's for beer and nachos on me."

"Tony's?" His dubious expression told me he'd never heard of it.

"I'm sure you've never been there and it's about time I took you to one of my favorite places. But they have a dress code. You'll want to lose your blazer. Thank God you have your jeans here."

He laughed and played along. It was good he had a drawer of casual clothes in my dresser. He nodded and followed me to the bedroom where he took off his button down collared shirt and put on a white T-shirt instead. He exchanged his work slacks for jeans, and I even got him to wear boat shoes, which was not something he ordinarily did.

We walked from my swanky new apartment twenty or so city blocks to my old neighborhood. The air was crisp but warmer than usual for an Ontario winter. I could tell Sebastian was ever so slightly uneasy as this was a part of the city with which he was unfamiliar. I appreciated his willingness to trust me. I held his hand and pointed out markers for him, like I was giving him a guided tour of a foreign land. That's where to get the best ice cream, over here is my acupuncturist, right down this lane was where I puked the first time I got drunk watching a hockey game. This was definitely *my* neighborhood and I became nostalgic at every turn. It was so fun to have Sebastian along to see it. We passed the Subway station, but the girl with the cat wasn't there. I made a mental note to share some of my newfound abundance with her one of these days.

We entered Tony's, a big brick building, constructed over a hundred years ago. Tony poked his head out from the kitchen and waved to me. Carla, our server, seated us and went over the specials but I told her we were here to celebrate and wanted a big plate of nachos and a pitcher of beer. Sebastian looked kind of awkward. What I wanted more than anything was to introduce him to my world. I had to be able to be myself around him.

"So, I'd like to take this opportunity to formally tender my resignation, Mr Porter," I said, raising my glass to his.

He looked taken aback. "What? Why?"

"Because I'm a woman of independent means. I always have been." My confidence poured out of me. I was grinning from ear to ear.

"Well, sure but…" he protested.

"Sebastian, I appreciate that you helped me through a hard time and thanks to your generous salary I was able to turn my life around after Pete. I'm grateful. And now I'm ready to stand on my own two feet."

"Are you sure?" He met my eyes as if to assure me that he would always be there for me.

"More than sure."

"All right. I accept your resignation." He glimpsed around the pub. "Actually, I'm proud of you. You have something I don't have."

"Oh?"

"Yeah. I admire your tenacity. You make great choices, Claudia."

"Well, I've been thinking a lot about what we've been talking about with relationships and it's crucial for my own peace of mind that I don't become reliant on you in any way."

"You letting me share my wealth with you is not the same as reliance."

"No, but I want to make sure I pay my own way in this life and I never want to let money influence our relationship. Besides, I can afford to take care of myself, so why wouldn't I?"

I felt powerful and satisfied. It was so good to sort out the economic ties between us, to free us up to having only a personal relationship. I would always treasure his gifts and the way he had set me up in the most deluxe home I could imagine. He refused to budge on the issue of the apartment, which he told me he'd bought as an investment. I insisted on paying rent, but he only charged me what my former landlord had.

When the bill came, Sebastian reached for it but he relented with a mere glance from me. This was the turning point.

"Thanks for a fun night out," he said.

"Tony's nachos are the best, eh?"

"Definitely. Who knew?" He put his paper napkin down on the table and motioned toward the door. "Shall we?"

He held the glass door open for me and we walked into the relatively balmy evening hand in hand.

"You are my dream woman," he said quietly as we descended the steps onto the tree-lined street.

"I am?"

"It's a dream come true for a guy like me to be with a woman as headstrong and resolute as you are. I love spending money on you, as you know, but the one thing about growing up with a lot of money was that it was sometimes hard to pick out who your real friends were, you know?"

"Well, in all seriousness, I don't want you for your money."

"I know that. That's why you're my dream woman. I feel like you see me for who I am and you actually like who I am."

"More than like."

"Really?"

"Sebastian, I am falling hard for you."

He took me in his strong embrace and kissed me heavily. Then he looked right into my eyes and said, "Claudia Richards, I am smitten with you."

My heart pounded so hard it seemed as though my chest could no longer contain it. I had butterflies in my tummy and the world was bathed in sunlight. We kissed again.

"I am smitten with you, too."

* * * *

During the day on Saturday, I went to the spa to treat myself to some pampering that I deserved on many levels. I was looking forward to having dinner with Sebastian and his wife and his wife's lover. The meeting coupled with my incredible promotion called for a pedicure, manicure, facial and massage. The works. I walked in at eleven in the morning. I didn't leave until four in the afternoon. My legs were waxed, I was scrubbed and kneaded all over. My nails were perfect. Everything was as good as it could be. I was still harboring some insecurities, but I forced myself to remember that I was about to meet some of the important people who had helped to shape Sebastian, the man I was falling for. It was highly likely that we'd get along with each other since we all cared about him.

I wore my best outfit—my dark-purple blazer with gray trousers and a white blouse. I wanted to summon the spirit of Katherine Hepburn. I was determined to make a good impression and feel great because at least when it came to matters of the heart, I was on track.

I buzzed and Anne Lise came to the door to greet me. From the entrée I could hear boisterous laughter and immediately felt nervous. She took my jacket and ushered me into the living room, part of me wanted desperately to turn back.

"Claudia," Sebastian said as he stood.

Deb and Hatia stood too as I walked toward them. I was grateful Sebastian had shown me photos so I knew right away who was who.

First impression of Deb—she was gorgeous, worldly, and looked great next to Sebastian. Her brown hair was cropped into a bob and she was draped in white, wearing a dress that also had a white cape. It was very fashionable. I felt mousy but tried to remind myself this wasn't a competition. I was here as

Sebastian's sweetheart. Maybe it was okay if I felt insecure around Deb.

"You must be Deb." I extended my hand.

She returned the gesture. Her hands were soft but her handshake firm.

Hatia seemed like she did not even understand the concept of insecurity. She had long dark hair tied back in a ponytail. Her features were accented by her stark hairstyle. She wore a rustic leather vest over top a pair of dark pants and white men's shirt. Around her neck, she had a rustic leather strand that held a gemstone talisman, which added to her mystique. It was easy to understand why Deb had needed to spend half of her time with her. She was everything one might expect a famous Spanish sculptor to be.

"And you must be Hatia." I shook her hand.

It was in that moment of assessment that I realized that Sebastian must have felt insecure about his wife wanting to be with a successful artist, that he must on some level be hurt by Deb's choice to be with the kind of artist he wished he was. I didn't believe he was happy with merely playing the role of benefactor, in spite of his insistence.

"Aren't you going to greet me?" Sebastian said, which naturally caused me to extend my hand to him only to see that he was leaning forward to kiss me. *Awkward.* I quickly lowered my hand and kissed him.

It was odd to have witnesses yet when Sebastian's lips touched mine, I forgot about everything else and concentrated on him. When we opened our eyes, I felt our familiar togetherness and that put me at ease. I was here to get to know two people who were important to him and that was all I needed to remember. I sat down on the loveseat next to Sebastian. The four of us were facing each other with a coffee table in between us that had three glasses of sparkling water and a bouquet of flowers. Anne Lise quickly showed up with an empty glass and the green bottle.

"Thanks," I said to her. She nodded.

"So, Claudia, it's nice to finally meet you," Deb said. "Sebastian has told me so much about you."

"Good, I hope," I said, trying to sound humble.

"Marvelous, actually," she said. "I haven't seen him so smitten before."

I gulped. Then I noticed Sebastian was shaking his head at her and blushing. He seemed embarrassed. It was so sweet. When he looked at me it was pure magic.

"Oh wow," Hatia observed. "Did you see those sparks? These two are on fire," she said to Deb but we were clearly meant to be included.

Were they trying to embarrass us? I couldn't tell. But my heart was on my sleeve. I was hiding nothing. I wanted Deb to realize that Sebastian was my everything. My heart was all in. And clearly it was the same for Sebastian. I felt so solid in our love.

"They sure have chemistry," Deb said back to Hatia.

I flashed a goofy smile at Sebastian who met my eyes for a split second before turning beet red and hiding his face in his right palm, while holding my hand with his left one.

"Deb, please," he said.

"What? I can't point it out? It's adorable, Sebastian. I'm happy for you."

Why was this so natural? Why were these two women so kind? I wasn't scared at all anymore and felt very much that I was welcome there.

"So, Claudia, tell us more about yourself."

"Well, I don't know what Sebastian has told you but I just got a new job."

"Oh?"

"I've been working on my PhD in Milton at the English department at the University of Toronto and TAing courses for the past few years. And just yesterday I was offered my own course. In September, I will officially be a professor teaching my own course."

"That's fantastic," Deb said. "Actually, Sebastian told us last night. Congratulations."

"Very impressive," said Hatia.

"I'm so proud of you," Sebastian said and he hugged me even though we were sitting down.

I think it was his way of putting his arm around me because he left it there and held onto me from then on. It was warm and good. I wanted him close.

"Thanks," I said to each of them.

It was huge news for me, but I didn't want to monopolize the conversation with it. I'd only just met them.

"Other than that, I am kind of boring," I said.

"I highly doubt that," Deb said.

"Really. I read a lot. I stay home a lot. Several years of working on my thesis made me pretty insular and now I'm just learning to be more balanced. Sebastian is helping me to see that there's a lot more to life than just books."

Sebastian squeezed my hand.

"Well you seem like a real gem to me," Deb said.

She was so kind. I kept waiting for her to say something catty but she didn't. To think that my whole life I'd thought of women as competitors instead of allies was disheartening to consider, but in the comfort of their home, I understood the real meaning of love. Deb was so sincere in her effort to get to know me. That was really beautiful to observe. She never made 'we' statements the way many married women do. She didn't make assumptions about Sebastian. It was novel to watch them interact, and I understood how letting go of the assumptions of monogamy didn't mean letting go of love. It was comforting to think of all the honest communication that must have taken place between these three people in order to accommodate what was truly in their hearts instead of what society expected them to be.

Once we progressed to dinner, it was like hanging out with friends I'd known forever. Hatia entertained everyone with her stories about the art scene in Barcelona and Deb shared her latest thoughts on current events. I was surprised that we had so much in common. She wasn't conservative the way I assumed most rich people were. She cared about unions and the working class and even talked about how much she wants to pay taxes, especially when they go toward good things.

Sebastian was fairly reserved all night. He had the wisdom to let the women figure each other out. I recognized that this was a conscious choice on his behalf because a couple of times he started to tell stories but stopped. I liked the generosity with which he listened.

After Anne Lise served dinner—a delicious pork roast with potatoes, gravy, a vegetable medley and stuffing—she announced that she was officially retiring for the evening and would clean up the following day. So once dinner was over, Deb and I took the dishes out to the kitchen and piled them into the sink. It was a rare opportunity to see the kitchen. It was massive and so well laid out. I wanted badly to explore it and could picture myself making delicious meals for Sebastian.

I was reminded of Sebastian's disclosure that Deb never cooked and I could tell she was uncomfortable even carrying dishes. She had perfectly manicured nails and several rings on each hand as if to declare to the world that she didn't belong in domestic settings.

I was about to go back into the dining room when Deb said, "Let's give Anne Lise a break and do the dishes together."

I was almost positive she'd never done dishes before in her life and there was a dishwasher in plain sight. She was just trying to think up an excuse to talk to me alone. I took the bait.

"Sure."

I opened the door beneath the sink and grabbed the dish soap, dish brush and gloves.

"Only one pair of gloves," I said. "You better take them."

"Thanks," she said and put them on.

"Do you want to wash or dry?" I asked.

She looked puzzled. "Oh, uh, dry."

So I ran the hot water over the plates and started to wash the dishes. She took off the gloves and passed them back to me.

"Sebastian is taken by you," she said.

"It's mutual," I said.

"Oh good. Then this should be easy. I really like you, Claudia. I'm glad that Sebastian has such good taste. He has a fondness for strong and like-minded women."

I could see how this was a very delicate tapestry we were weaving together. We would undoubtedly be seeing a lot of each other if Sebastian and I became a serious item. Holidays and vacations. It was important to fit in with the family.

"I wasn't sure what to expect but I like you," I said.

"Good. I don't want to stand in the way of anything." Then, ominously, she added, "I would if I had to but let's hope it never comes to that."

I said nothing and just continued to wash dishes. What had she expected me to say? The silent tension began. To disrupt the awkwardness I decided to take over the conversation thread.

"I am very loyal. I stayed with my last boyfriend far too long, actually. We were together for five years and I only left him because he gave me no other option."

"Why was that?"

"Well, he cheated."

"So you were monogamous?"

I nodded. "Yeah."

"I see."

I didn't want to ask her about the rules and boundaries and parameters of her relationship with either Hatia or Sebastian. We'd only just met after all. And I felt so inexperienced compared to them. My one major relationship had been quite traditional. And what a way to have it end. Cheating. How cliché, I thought. I hoped she wasn't judging me too hard for it.

"So, Claudia, do you want to get married and have kids some day?"

"I haven't decided yet."

"Oh?" She looked alarmed. "Sebastian said you didn't want either."

I was in a near panic. Had I really said that I didn't want either? I remembered saying something disparaging about marriage the first night we met, but kids? Hmmm.

We looked at each other. There was only one way this miscommunication had happened.

"Sebastian!" Deb yelled. "Would you come in here for a moment?"

Oh my God. This was not good. Sheepishly, Sebastian came into the kitchen as though he knew there was a scolding waiting for him.

"Sebastian, I'm trying to understand why you told me that Claudia doesn't want children or marriage."

"Well—" He looked at me and I could tell he was nervous. "Don't be mad. I think it was just a misunderstanding. My first impression was that she didn't."

"And then you learned that your first impression was incorrect but you decided not to tell me?"

He nodded.

"Sebastian, that is a huge breach of trust."

"I know. I'm sorry."

He held his head down. "I just knew if you two had a chance to meet, you'd hit it off and everything would work out perfectly."

"Well, we are hitting it off and I do like Claudia. I thought we had an agreement that Sarah would be an only child. Why did you lie?"

I wanted to disappear instead of being tangled in the web of two people who'd known each other since they were children. I looked down at the sudsy plates and continued to scrub as though to give space to Sebastian and Deb's conversation. I couldn't see myself as a mother, at least not yet, but it seemed a moot point.

"I just want everything to work out. I—I...this is not the way I wanted to say it."

"Say what?" I asked. I put the dish down and turn around to face Sebastian.

"Claudia, I love you."

I was shocked. Right here in front of his soon-to-be ex-wife in the middle of this tense moment. And it all fell away. It all just disappeared around us and we were back in our bubble of perfection. I hugged him. I held him so close. I wanted to jump up on him and wrap my legs around him but I restrained the desire.

"I love you, too," I whispered into his ear.

"Oh, brother," Deb said, shaking her head and rolling her eyes sarcastically. "I could tell from the first time you told me about her."

Just then Hatia came into the kitchen. I pulled away from Sebastian just a little but I wanted badly to be alone with him, to enclose ourselves in our bubble again and stay there. But I understood now how our relationship was not just ours but sometimes belonged to a larger network.

"Are you ready for dessert?" Hatia interjected. "I brought it from Spain but it needs a little time in the oven. Let me set it up."

"I'm going to go to my room for a few minutes," Deb announced.

"All right, sweetheart," Hatia said, putting her arms around Deb and kissing her cheek.

Somewhere deep inside, I trusted that it would all work out eventually. I could tell that it was strange for Deb to overhear a love declaration. I felt for her and I also felt the need to tell Sebastian I wasn't impressed with his timing but I was too blown away by the content of what he'd said. I knew Deb had not anticipated that our relationship was this intense. Considering we had not been dating that long, I was also shocked at how close we'd become. But I was in the middle of it and loving every minute. I didn't need to wrap my head around it.

"In that case, I'm going to take Claudia to see the painting I've started."

"You're painting again?" Hatia's face lit up. She seemed genuinely excited to talk with him about it.

"Yeah, there's so much we need to catch up on," he said warmly. "I'll tell you about it later."

Then Sebastian took me by the hand and led me back into the dining room where he looked at me and said, "I'm being a very bad almost-ex-husband right now. I need to go talk to Deb."

"Yeah, you should."

"I just… I'm so head over heels for you, Claudia. I'm forty-two and this is the first time I have felt this kind of passion."

"Well, that especially makes it wrong for you to spring the kid thing on her like that," I admonished. My voice was hushed. "Especially since I'm nowhere near ready."

"I know. I know," he said. "It was rash. But I'd rather get everything out in the open. Total honesty. I want her to know how important you are to me and that we're long term."

I was impressed that he was taking responsibility but sad on Deb's behalf that our first in-person encounter was so dramatic, and I hoped that we could make a better connection after this. I did feel so comfortable around her.

I went back into the kitchen and sat down while Hatia prepared the pastries she had brought from Spain. She must have sensed my nervousness because once she'd put the tray of goodies into the oven, she sat across from me and said, "I overheard everything from the dining room. Don't worry. They will sort this out."

"I wish he hadn't announced it like that."

"It'll be okay. I've never known those two to have a problem they couldn't sort out and I've known them for many years." She touched my arm gently as if to emphasize the need to relax. I probably exuded tension.

"I just really want this to work."

"Well, Deb does, too. So don't worry." Her smile reassured me.

"Can I ask you something?"

"Sure."

"Why are you poly?"

"Why? Let's see. It's been so long I've been like this I can't remember. I think it's the most honest form of relationship you can be in and as an artist, I need to be completely honest in everything I do because all lies compromise my creative integrity."

"So you think all monogamous people are liars?"

"No. I don't. But I think monogamy as a default paradigm is false. I definitely believe that there are monogamous people who are being completely true to their hearts. I just don't think that most people fall into that category and I've always wanted my own experiences to be honest and authentic and respectful."

She paused thoughtfully and I just listened. I wanted to hear everything she had to say because this was the opposite of what I grew up with and what I'd heard from Monique and my other girlfriends.

"Have you ever asked yourself why people cheat?" she asked. She opened the cupboard and took down a canister of loose leaf tea.

"Because they're assholes?" I couldn't help myself. Besides, I was thinking of Pete.

She laughed.

Phew.

"But that's a little simplistic, isn't it? Blaming the cheater creates a kind of victim mentality for the person who was cheated on."

"Yeah," I said. "I felt like a victim when I walked in on my boyfriend in bed with his ex."

"Oh, I'm sorry." She patted my arm again. "But why do you think he didn't tell you about her?"

"Honestly, it's been driving me crazy to analyze it. I guess something about our relationship made him feel like he couldn't tell me. We had been growing apart for years, actually. There was a lot I wasn't telling him, too, like how unhappy I was with our sex life and the mundane person I'd become."

"What do you mean?"

"Well, mousy. I kind of lost myself."

"First of all, you do not strike me as someone who could be dull, but I hear what you're saying about losing yourself. You lived together, right?"

I nodded.

"And it was your first serious live-in relationship?"

I nodded again. I felt like I could tell her anything.

"That happens. My first live-in relationship was like that, too."

"When was that?"

"Oh, ages ago now. We were both free spirits but it just seemed like moving in together was what people did."

"Oh, your first relationship was also with a woman?"

"Yeah. I've never been with a man. Well, other than Sebastian. I suppose you've heard about that fiasco." She laughed gregariously.

I laughed, too. It felt so intimate to be in on this secret the three of them shared.

"How long were you and the other woman together?"

"Four years," she said. "And I was cheating for the last two."

"Oh, then I'm sorry I said that cheaters are assholes," I said. I wasn't sure why I apologized. I still think cheating is horrendous, but I didn't want to offend her. I was her guest, too, and wanted to make a good impression.

"Well, I felt like an asshole at the time, so don't worry. I was young. I hadn't figured myself out yet. Nowadays I'd never agree to live a life constricted by another person's insecurities. But that's what our relationship was like back then. I wish I'd had the courage to be honest with her about my attraction to others but I felt like I couldn't tell her because she was very judgmental and extremely insecure and jealous."

"You know, sometimes I think I might be too insecure to ever try it."

"Wait a second. So you and Sebastian are monogamous?"

"I don't know. We haven't figured it out yet. My best friend gave me some books to read and I did and it sounds like it might be something to try but I don't know yet, and anyway, we only just started dating so, yeah, we haven't discussed it."

"Hmm. Well, you know I could see Sebastian going either way, to tell you the truth. He's a timid man deep in his heart, a loyal and humble man. He's a good one."

"I think so."

"Many people have a mistaken impression of him, I noticed when I first started coming here. Don't forget, when we first met, they came to me. Spain relaxed them. I find North Americans can be quite uptight. It's good for them to have a few weeks in the Spanish countryside now and then."

I nodded. "Well, that's true about being uptight over here. I can see that." It was exceedingly obvious in this very conversation, in fact. I laughed at myself on the inside. I did need to loosen up a bit and feel secure in my own skin. Sebastian was a good man and he had just told me he loved me. What a relationship with him and his family might look like, I didn't know, but it also didn't matter. I was so comfortable right here, right now.

"Well, anyway, Claudia," Hatia said with her hand on my arm, "you are young, that's true. But you don't strike me as insecure."

"Maybe I'm not. I am jealous, though."

"Jealousy is normal in poly relationships."

"It is?"

"Sure."

"But…how do you deal with it?"

"I consider all the blessings of being with people who are honest with themselves and with me. I expect that. I mean, the heart is a precarious thing. People fall in and out of love. People have crushes and people have sexual attractions and fantasies that don't turn into love relationships but do turn into beautiful manifestations of human desire. I remind myself that if I'm always honest about my emotions and I deal with people who are honest with theirs, then we can get through anything." She prepared the ceramic teapot by swirling hot water in it to warm up the porcelain. Then she scooped in some tea leaves and added boiling water.

"So you have other lovers besides Deb?"

"Sure." She smiled.

Suddenly, I could feel her magnetism. I could see exactly what other women saw in her. She was so insightful and attractive.

"Deb knows all of them," she continued. "Unless they're just one-time play mates. But if any kind of emotional connection develops, Deb meets them. She's my primary relationship so she has to know who I'm involved with."

"I see."

"This is all very new to you, isn't it?"

"Yeah," I admitted. I was afraid she'd judge me but I didn't feel like she was. Instead, I felt like she understood me.

"Well, life is a process and you make mistakes, for sure. I mean, in the future, you probably won't want to rush it if you meet someone who has been married as long as Sebastian and Deb."

"Yeah, I'm kind of catching on to that."

"But you couldn't ask for a better man to get involved with. And Deb is really supportive of everything Sebastian does and vice versa. They have an amazing connection. I guess that's what happens when two people get together so young. They've always been honest with each other. It's really beautiful."

"Yeah, it is." I nodded. I felt honored to hear Hatia's perspective. "I never realized that relationships could be like this."

"Most people don't."

"I still don't understand why they're getting divorced," I said. I felt immediately self-conscious since I probably should have asked Sebastian directly. This was clearly not a family that gossiped behind peoples' backs.

Hatia laughed in an animated way by flailing her arms in the air. "That's easy. It's because Deb and I are getting married."

We laughed. Just then, Deb and Sebastian came back into the kitchen. Sebastian had his arm around Deb but must have caught the last word.

"Who's getting married?"

Deb and Hatia eyed each other with panic-stricken faces, and I looked at Sebastian feeling totally clueless as to how to handle this.

Sebastian stepped back from Deb and stared at her inquisitively. She gave him a knowing glance and said, "Sebastian, we have something to tell you."

"What?" He seemed shocked, and I couldn't tell if it was in a positive or negative way but suddenly it felt weird that Deb had called him out earlier.

"Congratulations!" He hugged Deb and with a gesture summoned Hatia into a group hug.

I stood by, enjoying the way this night had turned out. Deb was the first to pull away as the group hug dispersed.

"Dessert ready?" Deb asked.

"Yes," Hatia said and went to the oven and turned it off. She pulled out the most beautiful-looking puff pastries and put them on a tray.

We all followed her back to the living room where we sat down. The evening ended with all the warmth with which it had started.

When Sebastian drove me home, I asked him what had happened with Deb's announcement.

"Why did you let her blame you for not being forthright? And then when she wasn't completely honest with you, you just accepted it."

"Wisdom, my dear."

"What?"

"I had to make a choice in that moment whether it mattered more to be right and to win an argument or whether it mattered more to be kind. I chose kind. They're family after all."

"Sebastian, you are one incredible man. I'm so lucky."

"I'm the one who's lucky. Claudia, I love you. I'll say it whenever and wherever I want, no matter who feels awkward about it."

"I love you, too."

He assured me everything was fine and would continue to get better the more we all got to know each other.

"She likes you," he concluded.

"I like her, too. And Hatia," I said. "Honestly, that was one of the best dinners of my life. I really like them both a lot."

"I'm so glad, Claudia," he said. "It's so rare to have a connection like you and I have and I want everything to be perfect. I apologize to you for making you feel awkward earlier."

"I accept your apology," I said sincerely. "Now, tell me again…those three little words."

"I love you."

"Again," I ordered.

He smiled. "I love you. I love you. I love you."

"I'll never get tired of hearing it. When did you know?"

"I want to say the very first night I met you but you wouldn't believe me."

"I felt something very intense that night too," I confessed. "It wasn't something I've ever felt before, either. And, actually, it scared me."

"Me too. Love can be scary."

He looked so vulnerable in that moment as we pulled into my parking garage.

"Do you want to come up?" I asked. "Or should you go home?"

"I'll come up."

"Deb isn't expecting you to come back, is she?"

"No, not tonight. I told her if you asked me to come in, I would."

I was so glad to hear he'd be staying the night. I couldn't wait to get him upstairs and express my love to him in words and in body.

Once in the comfort of my living room, we cuddled on the couch and kissed deeply. His kisses felt so much more intense now, like we'd both bared our souls to each other. There was nothing between us now that couldn't be spoken.

Chapter Eleven

The next time I visited the house was for dessert after Sebastian had asked me to accompany him to a corporate dinner function. He had recently begun to open up about just how much he didn't like going to such events and how much better it was with me on his arm. When we arrived back at the Porter mansion, Sebastian took my hand and led me up the staircase. He took me down the hall but we didn't turn into his studio. Instead he kept leading me until we were in his bedroom. I hadn't been in here before and it suddenly struck me that my lover was incredibly private. A different type of girl might have harangued him to see it sooner, but with Sebastian patience was key.

"This is where I come to get away from everything and everyone. I never bring anyone into this space," he said.

"Never?" *Too weird!*

"Until now. I've been wanting to show you for a while." Still holding my hand, he flipped a switch that turned on a few small lamps around the otherwise dark room.

There were plants and paintings, a massive bookshelf filled with books and an antique desk with a fitting old-fashioned chair. In the corner was a huge brown and beige globe on a wooden stand with brass trim. For some reason, I'd pictured him sleeping in a king-sized bed, like the one back at the Fairmont in Calgary, but instead there was a humble day bed tucked into a nook. On the nightstand next to it was Milton's Paradise Regained. I went to it immediately and, picking it up, saw that his bookmark was near the end.

"Seriously?" I asked. It made my heart melt that he shared my interest. He probably didn't actually, but what floored me was his willingness to try. "If I were a man, I'd want my man cave to look like this," I said.

He laughed. "I tend to think of it as a bedroom. I like your description more."

"Surely you let your family come in here," I said.

"Only in case of emergency."

"Anne Lise?"

"Ditto."

"Sebastian Porter, you are one complex guy."

"That about sums it up," he said, "but I want you to have access. I want you to know all of me."

"In that case, can I see your new painting?"

"In good time," he said. Then he grabbed me and pulled me into him. "Right now, there's something else I want to show you."

"What's that?"

"This." He lifted me up and I wrapped my legs around him as I'd wanted to do when I was over last time. We couldn't then. It would have been inappropriate, but tonight I wasn't meeting the family.

Tonight, I was just over. He pressed his hard cock against me. I could feel it through all of the layers of clothing between us.

"You wanted to show me your erection?" I giggled.

"I wanted to show you how much I want you, how much I love you, how I need to have you."

He unzipped his pants. I could not believe it. Right here? Right now? There were two women—one of whom was still technically his wife—waiting for us downstairs. This was so wrong, so bad. So hot!

"Sebastian, don't you think they'll know?" I whispered.

He shook his head. "I don't care," he said. "I need to feel you. I need to be inside you right now. I need you to know how I feel about you and this is the best way I have of communicating that. Now take off your panties."

This was so unexpected. I was shocked to feel the response my clit gave his words. His urgency made me instantly wet. I couldn't believe it but it was true. My pussy wanted him badly. Years of social conditioning and knowing my manners had made me deny what my body wanted. It was good to give in. This was our moment, after all.

Before I knew it, Sebastian was lying flat on his back, his pants along with his boxers were down around his knees. Only his cock and thighs were exposed. And I was still wearing my dress. My panties were still suspended around my left ankle when I propped myself up over him and gently lowered my pussy to his cock while we kissed. He thrust his cock in me. It was primal and hot. I could tell how desperately he wanted me because he didn't go slow, didn't stop to check in with me. Instead, he fucked me. Hard. He gripped firmly onto my hips as he prompted my movements, lifting and lowering me as he drove his cock deeper. The shock of it was so mind-blowingly hot. Everything about his lack of ability to control himself turned me on.

"Oh, yeah," I whispered into his ear. "I love the way you fuck me."

"I love fucking you. I love you, Claudia."

And just like that, the beastly part of him and the beautiful gentle side of him merged into one. I was complete with him. The overwhelming joy of our union allowed me to completely surrender to him.

"I love you, too, Sebastian. Now fuck me."

And he did. He pumped his cock in and out until our bodies made slapping sounds that were unmistakable, and I said a little prayer that nobody would come looking for us because they'd know for sure what we were up to. *Slap, slap, slap.* My thighs against his. His cock inside me. And then, with his face distorted from intensity, Sebastian told me he was about to come. Moaning, he pulled down on my hips, pushed his cock deep and released. The throbbing feeling of his cock filling me up was all I could take. I flicked my clit with my middle and forefinger with his cock still pulsating in my ravenous cunt. My clit gave way to a powerful orgasm. I lowered myself down to lie on Sebastian's chest as we savored surrendering to our lust for each other.

We were horizontal on the day bed, snuggled together. "I love you, Claudia Richards."

"I love you, too, Sebastian Porter."

* * * *

Downstairs, Hatia and Deb had set the table for dessert. These folks knew how to live. As soon as they realized we were home, there was ice cream on the table, along with a trivet for whatever was about to come out of the oven. It smelled fantastic, whatever it was. And there was coffee.

"Please, sit down." Deb gestured to a chair.

I followed her lead and sat down, hoping that my face wasn't flushed and sweaty as it had appeared in the upstairs bathroom mirror when I'd cleaned up. I had successfully avoided all mirrors on the way down. My mind raced with images of Sebastian and me in his room, two impossibly horny people with no ability to control themselves.

Sebastian sat across from me but yet I couldn't look at him. It was like we were naughty children or something.

"So what do you think of Sebastian's painting?" Hatia wanted to know.

"I'm not allowed to see the new one yet," I said. It was the truth.

"When did you get your creative mojo back?" she asked him.

"It was Claudia," he said, his tone suddenly serious. "She inspired me. We had a great trip to Malcolm's opening in Calgary and our conversations about art made me realize that I had something new to explore."

"Ah. Malcolm. How is that bad boy?" Hatia's eyes lit up as though she were thinking something scandalous.

"He's good. Sends his love."

Hatia raised an eyebrow. I wondered what had happened there. But she didn't say anything about it. Instead, she picked up on their previous conversation.

"I couldn't sculpt for five years once. Then, one day, I was out on my uncle's boat with him in the Alboran

Sea and I caught a fish and as I was reeling it in, it came back. That desire. Inspiration."

"It's so interesting that you're both artists," I said, looking at Hatia.

"Isn't it? Yes. I've always thought so. Deb has a type." She winked. Hatia was so charismatic. I understood the attraction perfectly.

"Oh stop," Deb said to Hatia, seeming shy all of a sudden.

"Claudia, what are you doing tomorrow?" Deb queried, likely as a way of changing the subject.

"I don't have plans."

"Would you like to spend the day together? I'm driving out to St. Mary's with a care package for Sarah. I'd like you to meet each other."

"Um. Sure."

Yikes. My anxieties arose again.

"Great. That'll give Hatia and Sebastian some time alone to discuss art."

"Great."

It must have been pretty vulnerable for Deb to be far away and not know what was going on at home. It must also have made her vulnerable to accept a stranger into her family life, to take the risk. And I looked at her with gratitude and appreciation for her hospitality toward me.

That night, Sebastian drove me home. When we got to my apartment, I invited him up.

"I better not," he said.

"Why not?"

"I'm kind of tired."

"No way, mister. You don't get to give me a quick poke in the man cave, get me all hot and heavy and then drop me off without finishing what you started."

"Oh, it's like that, is it?"

"It is," I said, my tone surprisingly dominant.

"Well, I wouldn't want you to go home unsatisfied."

"That's more like it. Now park the car and let's go upstairs."

I stared at his face. Here in front of me was this perfect man, this generous and loving, wonderful man. And we could be together. Any obstacles I'd seen before were in my head.

I nodded. "How do you think it will go with me meeting Sarah?"

"Don't be nervous. Just let Deb take the lead on how she introduces you."

"What do you mean?"

"She might refer to you as my friend. I don't want you to be offended. It's hard to be a teenager. Deb and I decided it's way too hard to be a teenager with polyamorous parents so we're keeping her in the dark, at least until she's old enough to understand."

"When will that be?"

"When she's fifty."

"Sebastian." I playfully shook my head. "You can't protect her forever."

"No, that's true. But she's got enough to worry about with school and we both want to see her reach her goals of getting into a top notch university before we burden her with any of our sordid details."

"So what about Hatia?"

"Oh, you mean Mom's best friend? Sarah loves her. She visits them in the summers sometimes."

"And she doesn't know?"

"She knows they're a couple, but not about their open relationship. She's wrapped up in her own world. She's got her studies to think about."

"And boys."

"No. She's at an all-girls school."

"Sebastian, you're being downright naïve."

"Well, we haven't heard anything about any boys yet."

"So when are you going to mention the divorce? At Deb and Hatia's wedding ceremony?"

"Claudia, just leave it to us. We're her parents. We'll decide what she should know and when."

Instantly I remembered exactly why this was a dangerous game to play, this game of belonging in their home, belonging in their family. If it had been unclear before, I knew how badly I wanted to belong now.

"I don't know how to fit into this," I said.

"It takes time to figure these things out. We've only just begun."

"Yeah, and Deb and Hatia could tell from a mile away that we're in love. Don't you think Sarah will notice?"

"She might."

"And then what? You'll just insist that I'm your friend?"

"I don't know, Claudia. Please. Why are you making problems we don't even have yet?"

We got out of the elevator and walked to my door. I swiped my card, as though I was at a hotel. This apartment building was so high tech.

"I just—" But I couldn't finish the sentence. "Maybe you should just go home."

"No way. Not like this."

"I'm fine, really."

"You're not and I'm not leaving."

Inside, the lights came on automatically to a dim setting. We took off our coats and scarves and I wrestled with my knee-high leather boots.

"Come here," Sebastian said.

I squeezed myself against him. He wrapped his arms around me. I wanted everything to be perfect. I just had reservations. I wasn't so sure about how it would all work out. And maybe he was right that it was too soon to be upset about it. Maybe I just needed to keep an open mind like I had with Deb. I told him so and he agreed to tell Sarah that I was his girlfriend, not his best friend. I told him I'd stay out of parenting decisions, except where they impacted me. And eventually it would all make sense. One thing definitely did make sense and that was the feeling I had in his arms. It was comforting and warm. But it was also an incredible turn on.

"I trust you," I said.

"I want us to work."

"Me too."

"I want you. You're everything I've been waiting my whole life for. I feel like I've undergone some excellent training in my marriage. If you'd met me when I was just starting out, you'd know. I was clueless about women."

"You're certainly not clueless anymore."

"Oh no?" he asked in a seductive voice.

"Not at all," I purred. "Come here."

I took him by the hand and led him to my bedroom. In the silence of the dark room, I sat him down on the edge of my bed.

There was light in the hallway but no direct light on me, so I felt comfortable to do something I'd never done before. I slowly started to take off my dress by unzipping it down the side seam.

"Oh wow."

In my most seductive voice, I asked Sebastian to help me out of it. He held onto the dress while I pulled it off. Then I was down to my bra, panties and garter with nylons.

"Oh my God," Sebastian said. "I didn't know you had stockings like this on."

"How do think we were able to have our naughty tryst?"

"I didn't think about it."

"Bad boy. You have no idea what lengths a lady will go to for you."

"What can I do to make it all better?"

"Hmm. Let's see," I said. "Well, you could take my panties off and give me a big huge orgasm with your tongue."

"Gladly."

He got up and grabbed hold of me then tossed me onto the bed. I fumbled my way up to the pillows and spread my legs open to give him access.

"Your pussy is the most tantalizing pussy in the whole world. It's all I can think about. I had to have you today, you know. That was not a choice. It was a need."

"I see. Well, I understand the need."

"You do?"

"I most certainly do. My pussy also needs to be satisfied, you see."

"I always want to satisfy your pussy's needs."

"Good." I handed him a pillow.

He took the hint and placed it next to my pelvis. I lifted myself up as he slid the pillow beneath my hips. Then, he got on his knees and lowered his head. His tongue touched the opening of my cunt, and immediately I was aware of my wetness.

He slowly licked me from the bottom of my pussy to the top.

I settled into the sensation while he explored me. I was so turned on but I didn't want to come yet. I had another plan for that. I ordered him onto his back and propped him up on the pillow while I straddled his chest. Then, using the headboard for balance, I sat on his face. It was like he was hugging my bottom the way he held me there, suspended just at his mouth level as he continued to lick my pussy.

The new angle gave me so much more control and I bobbed along with his movements and we quickly found a rhythm that worked for us. My clit was eager for release and just when I thought I was about to climb the mountain to the climax of relief, Sebastian unzipped his pants. His cock was so hard it sprang forth from the fly and without even bothering to help him take his pants off, I lowered my soaking wet pussy onto him. This was so dirty. I'd be leaving my mark everywhere and that was something primal in me, something deeply beast-like. I rode him hard. My pussy was ready to come, and I wanted nothing more than to reach my climax. He squeezed my nipples through my bra and the sensations pushed me over the edge. I moaned loudly and pressed myself onto him as hard as I could and then the muscles in my cunt began their familiar rhythms and I stopped all movement to savor the feeling. He must have been close too because just then he released his cum deep inside me and again I felt the throbbing of his cock as he ejaculated.

This time, I hopped off right afterward and took his cock into my mouth, hoping to feel one final burst as I cleaned him up. I loved the feeling of his spent cock in my mouth, the way it felt to let him relax there, let him trust me to take care of his cock.

"Sebastian, you dirty man."

He looked at me innocently. "I'm a bad boy. You said so yourself."

I flopped down next to him and he cradled me in his arms. "I love you," I said.

"I love you, too." He traced my body with his hand as he held me.

His gentle caresses sent shivers all over. In this relaxed state, I absorbed his touch like it was all that mattered.

Shortly after our post-coital nap, he zipped up his pants and sat up. "Time to go."

"So soon?"

"You have a big day tomorrow. I want you to be well rested."

"Okay."

I followed him to the door and we kissed tenderly once more. Before he left, he reached into his jacket pocket and pulled out a box. Although I'd never seen a box like that in real life before, I recognized it instantly from the billboards. It was from Tiffany's.

"Sebastian?"

"Just a little something."

"But…"

"Congratulations, Professor."

I opened the box and inside I found a pair of gold studs with a diamond setting.

"Oh, Sebastian." I was floored. Completely and utterly not expecting this.

"They're enchantment flowers, the shop girl told me. All the rage this year, apparently."

"I love them."

"And I love you."

We kissed again. I'd never been so celebrated before. Clutching the box to my chest, I felt so mushy inside it

was like I was going to implode from the good
feelings.

* * * *

After I closed and locked the door, I turned around
and surveyed the fantastic landscape that had become
my life. These beautiful clean lines, this dream
apartment, this modern minimalist furniture. It was as
though I had been lifted out of my old reality entirely.
I'd done a complete transformation. It was just after
eleven. I could still call Monique.

"You're not going to believe it," I said as soon as she
answered.

"What?"

"Sebastian told me he loves me."

"Get out!"

"Yeah, and Deb and Hatia are awesome. I totally like
them."

"Get back to the three little words."

"Well, it happened at dinner the first time I met
them, so it's all kind of wrapped up in the same
story."

"Spill it."

I told her everything and reliving it made it feel so
much more romantic and amazing. It was
unconventional, yes. It was not what Monique would
have wanted exactly, sure. But it was *my* romance. It
was my ideal relationship unfolding before me and I
loved it. I realized in that conversation that I didn't
need to justify anything to anyone, that all
relationships were unique and that if something
worked, then who cared what the world thought? I
realized my own complicated feelings about marriage
and children were nowhere near as important as the

connection we had. I spilled my thoughts on Deb and Hatia, how I understood their connection and how comfortable they had made me feel.

I curled up on the sofa with my earrings on the coffee table, in clear view. Talking on the phone like teenagers was divine. An hour and a couple of glasses of merlot later, Monique let the proverbial cat out of her secret bag.

"Jerome finally called me."

"Oh?" I realized I'd been so fixated on telling her my own news I hadn't even inquired what was going on with her.

"Yeah. He asked me to meet him for drinks last night so we could talk."

"So did you go?"

"I did."

"And?"

"The whole reason he transferred me was because he has feelings for me."

"Seriously?" I had butterflies on her behalf. Could it be that we were both going to find love?

"Yeah. And then he wanted to know what I thought."

"So you told him you're in love with him?"

"Not exactly, but I told him I was hurt that he transferred me and I missed him terribly."

"Okay, still true, just not the whole truth."

"Well I wasn't sure what his intentions were."

"And did you find out?"

"Uh-huh. He said since we're not working together anymore, maybe we could go out sometime. So I said how about next Saturday. I would have asked him for tonight but that just seemed too eager."

"Good girl. Play it cool. Well done."

"You think? I don't know. Now I kind of wish I'd just invited him back to my place right then and there."

"Showing some restraint is probably a good thing."

"I guess. Oh my God. What am I going to wear on Saturday? Maybe I can borrow one of your dresses."

"Anytime."

I hadn't heard Monique this thrilled in a long time. She deserved it. After so many years of her kissing frogs, I wanted nothing more for my best friend than a prince she could call her own. I knew deep down that Jerome had feelings for her. What man wouldn't? Men that Monique didn't even notice were in love with her. I could only imagine when she poured it on thick. Jerome was a sitting duck.

* * * *

The next day, Deb arrived exactly as scheduled at nine in the morning. We stopped for lattes on our way out of town and then hit the highway. On the road, we had a chance to talk more. I confessed I was afraid of meeting her and uneasy about their poly history at first, because I didn't know what it implied for me and Sebastian but that now I was more open-minded. It seemed as though she had anticipated that because she gave me the long version of what led them to open up their marriage to begin with.

"Sebastian and I practically had an arranged marriage. I mean we knew each other since we were children. Our parents are friends. We did what was expected of us and I'm glad, too, because you hear about some marriages that just don't work and I think it has a lot to do with family compatibility. But we were just kids when we got married and I already knew back then that I was attracted to women and I had no intention of living a chaste and monogamous life so you could say it was my bisexuality that prompted us to try this lifestyle."

"Yeah, Sebastian told me about the encounter with Hatia." I was trying to be as diplomatic as I could. And actually Hatia had told me, too.

"He told you?" she said, laughing. "Oh, he was a good sport about that. I know it wasn't easy for him. You just never know how things will turn out once sex gets involved."

"I guess." I had no idea. Or maybe I did because if it hadn't been for insanely hot sex with my handsome boyfriend, I wouldn't be driving out to a boarding school in the country with my boyfriend's co-parent. So I said, "Yeah. Sex definitely motivates us to do things we ordinarily wouldn't."

"You know, Sebastian is pretty private."

"I noticed."

"I've been wanting him to find a woman for a long time."

"Really?"

"That's what I told him I wanted for him. It was me who encouraged him to go for you, you know."

"I know."

"I just want you to know that I think Sebastian made a wise choice with you."

"Thank you." I was so shocked at how good her approval made me feel.

And then we pulled into Sarah's school. It was covered in ivy and had that stately air of sophistication one would expect of the most prestigious private boarding school in the country. My palms started to sweat and I felt enormously out of place being the third-wheel in this mother-daughter reunion.

We parked in front of the old brick building and Deb sent a text message. A few minutes later, a blonde teenager in a plaid skirt was running toward us. Deb got out of the car.

"Mom!" She hugged Deb.

"Sarah. Look at you, growing up so fast." They shared a sweet moment.

"I'd like you to meet a friend. This is Claudia."

We shook hands. "It's a pleasure," I offered.

"Why didn't Dad come?"

"He's painting again."

"Seriously? Awesome! He was so depressed for a while there."

"Not anymore."

"So what'd you bring me?" Sarah had a coy look in her eye.

Deb gave her a stern look then opened the trunk. There were two big shopping bags with boxes from shoe stores and some folded clothes. "Would I go to Spain for three whole months and not bring back some designer wear for my favorite daughter?"

"Thanks!" She grabbed the bags and started rifling through the items.

Deb shook her head at the sight and looked at me and shrugged. I was completely new to this style of parenting and realized that our worlds were different in a lot of ways and that Sebastian was right—it would take a while before I could justifiably share opinions about how he and Deb should raise Sarah. She seemed rather well adjusted from what I could tell, but it was hard to determine since she was busy holding up boots and scarves her mother brought her.

We had lunch together in the cafeteria, and Sarah showed me her room that she shared with a very sweet roommate. It looked like a lot of fun to live at a boarding school but when I pointed it out, Sarah assured me it was very challenging and that the administrators were strict. She had Sebastian's eyes and smile.

And that's when it all clicked into place for me. This was his family. These people meant the world to him. I no longer secretly wished they didn't exist. People have histories. I have a history, too.

When it was time to go, Sarah hugged her mom, and to my surprise she hugged me too and told me it was great to meet me. I told her it was mutual. As we left the idyllic campus, I felt a calmness come over me. This was Sebastian's family.

Once we were on the main road headed back, Deb asked whether I'd had a good time.

"It was wonderful," I said and meant it. "Sarah is a great girl."

She glanced over at me. "I'm glad you think so. I love Sebastian very much. And you know as well as I do that what he and I share is very different from what he has with you."

"I know."

"And, you know, I have a lot of respect for what he's building with you. I want you to be a part of our lives."

"I'm so glad."

We relaxed into the drive and listened to some classical music on the stereo. I understood how profoundly my life had shifted. It had been true what Sebastian said. I felt so much freer than I ever had before. It would still take some finessing to figure out how to tell my parents that the love of my life came with a package deal, but I was pretty sure that if they met the package, they'd understand. I couldn't wait to get back to the house so I could wrap my arms around Sebastian and tell him, yet again, how much I loved him.

Chapter Twelve

The following Tuesday, I met up with Monique for a quick lunch at the Market. We each got our meals and found a table in an area that wasn't too crowded. It felt like things were moving fast and each time we met up there were so many new things to tell. She looked radiant and happy and I had a feeling there was a new chapter, but I couldn't help but report first.

"You're not going to believe what happened last night," I started, hoping that Monique would comment on the earrings.

"Neither are you," she said. And her smile revealed that there was plenty more to hear.

"You first, then," I insisted.

"Well, um, let's see. Where do I begin?" Monique had that smug satisfied Cheshire cat grin that I'd been missing for the past few months. She was definitely back to her old self, which meant everything was coming up roses. She continued, "Well, Jerome and I finally met up."

"He called?"

"Nope. I called him to ask why he hadn't called."

I laughed. Classic Monique.

"So we talked on the phone for forty-five or so and then he asked what I was doing for dinner and I said I didn't have plans so he asked if I'd be interested in coming over since he was preparing his specialty — chicken kiev — for his...get this...his son."

"What?"

"Yeah. That's what I said."

"Since when does he have a kid?"

"Since six years ago. He kept it quiet at the office. He told me last night he didn't want people looking at him differently. He wanted to be open to travel and promotions that might include relocating."

"So he's not involved with the mother?"

"Mothers," she corrected.

"What?"

"He helped out his lesbian friends and they've got Aidan full time, but when he started going to Kindergarten he heard all these stories about daddies and started to wonder about his so the moms called Jerome and asked if he wanted to get involved. He hadn't found anyone to settle down with and he'd been curious about him so he'd said yes. Ever since then, for the past few years, he's had him over once a month for dinner and a sleep over. Isn't that the sweetest thing you ever heard?"

"I guess it is," I said, mostly responding to how happy Monique came across. It was odd, but I could see how it'd be neat, too.

"I met him last night and he's adorable."

"Whoa. Ms No Maternal Instincts. What happened to you?"

"I know, right? It's weird. But now I get it. I understand why Jerome was kind of cagey and secretive about his personal life. We all had dinner together and then we took Aidan to the park and he ran off and played. Jerome and I sat down and, I don't know, I just fell for him all over again."

I rolled my eyes. "You're incorrigible."

"I am. And he's so incredible. He's everything I want."

"Does he want more kids?"

"He's not sure. He says he's happy to have Aidan and he'd be satisfied to just have him, so…"

"Ideal!"

"I know!" Monique finished chewing a bite of her salad then she looked at my ears and said, "Check out this bling. Spill it, sister."

I blushed immediately. Even in front of Monique. It felt so fast all of a sudden, like I'd found my soul mate and wanted to shout it from the mountain tops.

"They're from Sebastian. His congratulations present for my new job."

"That was sweet of him."

I nodded. "He's the sweetest guy I've ever known."

"Oh, would you look at us. Who would have thought even a few months ago that this is where we'd be?"

I shook my head in amazement. "Tell me about it. A few months ago, I was still Frumpzilla."

"We sure killed her off!" Monique laughed.

"Yep. She's gone."

"Like a snake that's shed its skin."

"Well, technically, Frumpzilla is the skin, not the snake."

"Pardon me, professor," Monique said in her mocking tone. "Speaking of which, I have a little surprise of my own. It's not diamond earrings, but here." She reached into her purse and pulled out a tiny box, also from Tiffany's.

"Oh my God. What's this?"

"Open it."

I gasped. Inside was a silver locket in the shape of a heart. When I pried open the little encasement, I found a tiny picture of me and Monique in high school, taken on one of the happiest days we'd had together. We had our arms around each other in a photo booth picture we'd taken at the mall. She must have shrunk it down to size. On the other side of the heart was the photo she'd taken of us on the night I'd met Sebastian. On the back, it said *friendship is forever*. Immediately tears ran down my cheeks. I threw my arms around her and felt the warmth and trust and safety that was between us. I never would have made it through if not for Monique.

"I love you so much," I whispered in her ear. "You know, men come and go but you and I are forever."

"I love you too, Claudia. You're my best friend in the world." She sat back down on her seat and I could see that she had also started to shed some tears, her eyes pink and liquidy. "But I gotta say, I don't think these men will be going anywhere any time soon."

"Amen!" I blurted. "But in all seriousness, what would I have done without you?"

"Yeah, I don't know. You'd have been doomed to wear that danged old faded black turtleneck forever. Tell me you've thrown that thing out by now."

"Um..."

"Claudia, for God's sake. You've got a whole new wardrobe."

"It's a reminder. I need it."

"But you're not wearing it any time soon, are you? Please say no."

"I won't. I promise."

"You are so much more fabulous than that. From now on, it's all fabulousness and zero frump-factor for you. Especially since you've got your sexy new position."

"I don't know if being a professor is sexy."

"Are you for real? It's the hottest. Better than being a sexy librarian. You have to know that."

"Really?"

"Hell yeah. You think Sebastian just wants you for your body? Gorgeous as you are, it's what's up here that he's in love with." She tapped the side of her temple.

Epilogue

Six happy months later...

Instructed to show up two hours early, I knocked on the door to Grunt Gallery on Spalding Avenue at seven. There were no lights on, even though it was already dark out. Sebastian opened the door. When he saw me, he said, "I'm so glad you're here."

"It's your opening. I wouldn't miss it."

"Come in, come in." He seemed nervous, which made sense. Nobody had seen the paintings yet, not even Deb or Hatia. The gallery owner, was the only one and he had made such a big deal about honoring Sebastian's wish to keep everything secretive. Even the pamphlets that advertised the event didn't show Sebastian's work, only a photo of him at his canvas, taken by me. When we took that photo the canvas was blank except for a few simple lines. Anything could have happened since then.

Sebastian called into the darkness, "My girlfriend Claudia is here."

It felt so good to hear him utter that. I loved being Sebastian's girlfriend. I wasn't his wife. I wasn't the woman with whom he co-parented. I wasn't a friend, I was his girlfriend and everyone knew it.

Gustav, the owner, a thin, well-dressed man, emerged from the corridor adjacent to the main gallery space. He greeted me by kissing both of my cheeks.

"She is as beautiful as you described," he said to Sebastian.

Sebastian smiled. I blushed.

"Are you ready to see my paintings?"

"Yes."

"Okay, before I turn the light on, I just want to say one more time that I love you, that you are one of my dearest soul mates in this life and I treasure every second I get to spend with you."

I felt weak in my knees. It was incredible, looking back, to think about where I'd been and where I was now. Soon this room would be packed with the arts crowd, the familiar faces from various functions, the people from the university and Sebastian's painter friends. Deb and Hatia would arrive fashionably late. Sarah would come wearing all black with dark lipstick, a profound shift from her regular uniform but she so seldom got to make her own fashion choices. Monique would make an entrance, dressed in her hot pink gown, the one I'd worn the night I'd met Sebastian. She'd have Jerome on her arm and an engagement ring on her finger. The band would play jazz, people would mingle, drink red wine, converse about the work and the night would be written up in the paper as a roaring success.

But before all of that, there was this moment, this glorious and remarkable moment when the man of my dreams held me tight in a dark, cold room and told me he loved me. He turned on the lights and I could see that he was telling the truth. Every painting was of me. Everywhere I looked I saw my own image reflected back at me.

"What do you think?" Sebastian asked.

"I'm shocked."

"Why? Didn't I tell you that you were my inspiration?"

"I didn't think you were being literal."

"They are magnificent," Gustav said. "And you can't argue with me because I know."

"I won't argue." I said. "They are beautiful."

"Like you," Sebastian said.

* * * *

After the opening, we all went back to my place. Sebastian was the man of the evening, but he didn't want any fuss to be made about him. The opening was over as far as he was concerned, and so was his moment in the spotlight. He joined me in the kitchen where we hauled out the lovely canapés and treats we'd ordered from a delightful little catering company. Monique and Jerome were on the patio enjoying the view of the city. Jerome had his arm around Monique, and although I could only see their backs, they were adorable.

My parents were in the living room, chatting with Sarah. It had taken them a couple of months to warm up to the idea that I was in love with a man who already had a child but once they'd met Sarah, they had been ready to spoil her like their own grandchild, though for them that didn't mean with name brand items. Instead they wanted to talk to her about school and her life and interests. It was pretty obvious that she was equally enamored with them. Deb and Hatia lounged in the sofa, and joined in the conversation with Sarah and my parents. Our other guests, mostly acquaintances, mingled about and enjoyed themselves.

In the kitchen, in the middle of this grand party, I was overcome with a sense of bliss. My life had come together. All the elements were here. I was whole and complete and loved for me. I grabbed Sebastian's waist and squeezed him tightly. He kissed the top of my head and thanked me for putting on such a fine party. I got tears in my eyes because I knew Sebastian saw me in a way I didn't even see myself. He accepted everything about me, even the stuff I had wanted to hide. I'd never tell Monique this, but he even told me he loved me in my ratty old turtleneck when I wore it one laundry day.

"Sebastian?" I asked.

He looked at me, noticed the tears and immediately asked, "What's wrong?"

"Nothing," I said. "Just tears of joy. I want you to know how much I love you."

"I love you, too."

"This is everything I ever wanted."

He hugged me. And, in the midst of all my favorite people, we kissed.

About the Author

Romance heroines have saved my sanity numerous times through break-ups and life changes. I find escaping into a romance both soothing and revitalizing—and even better when there are some steamy scenes to tantalize the imagination.

For most of my adult life, I've concentrated on carving out a serious career, but a number of love-hungry, sassy characters keep taking over my mind, insisting that I daydream, live vicariously through them and tell their stories. Watching these women emerge on the page gives me a different sort of satisfaction than I get from my day job. It is a joy to share them with readers.

I live in a tiny apartment in a crowded city and I like to think there is something romantic about this. I did manage to find my soul mate here.

Destiny Moon loves to hear from readers. You can find her contact information, website details and author profile page at http://www.totallybound.com.

Totally Bound Publishing